This book is dedicated to my parents, Vincent and Eula Coston, my late Uncle Juney who taught me that all things are possible, and the love of my life…you know who you are…

She's

Killin'

Me

a novel by **Alicia Coston**

Indigo Press

I
Indigo
Press

This book is a work of fiction. Names, characters, places and incidents are products of the author's imagination or are used fictitiously. Any resemblance to actual events or locales or persons, living or dead, is entirely coincidental.

Published by Indigo Press

ISBN: 0-9795100-0-7

First Indigo Press paperback edition September 2007

Manufactured in the United States of America

Remove thy way far from her, and come not nigh the door of her house: lest thou give thine honor unto others, and thy years unto the cruel. Lest strangers be filled with thy wealth; and thy labors be in the house of a stranger.

Proverbs 5:8-10

Prologue

I never imagined waking up naked in the back seat of a 2006 Mercedes CL 500, but I knew if hell felt like that, I was going to say my prayers every night if I made it home. I couldn't tell if tears or blood trickled from the corners of my eyes—the familiar taste of iron teasing the tip of my tongue quickly answered that question. Slowly, I gained consciousness. The harsh, fluorescent glare of an overhead light peeked beneath my blindfold.

My wrists and ankles were bound, and the twine was a python biting into my flesh. I shifted my right hip to lie on my side, giving my leather-burned dick some relief. Funny that at that very moment, I pictured Constance wrapping her thick lips around it to cool me off—she was the same bitch who had landed me in the back seat. The searing gashes in the back of my head began to throb again, and I blacked out.

$$$$

Connie stood in front of me. The room we were in was seemingly one big shadow. A spotlight shone down upon her from someplace I couldn't detect. Her entire body was laden with metallic green scales—she resembled a snake with full breasts, hips, and lips. Connie flicked her forked tongue out at me, and I winced. I was still bound by ropes, but to a chair this time.

A cool draft caressed my groin, and I realized I wore nothing from the waist down. My dick hung limply but began to harden as the light pursued her naked body down to the black marble floor. She slithered towards me, and before I could blink, she was in between my legs.

Connie hissed and her jaws snapped open, revealing two very long and sharp fangs. I closed my eyes, sensing that she was going to clamp her lips around my dick—I knew it would be the most immense pain I could ever fathom. It turned out to be the complete opposite. When I opened my eyes again, this beautiful, bronze goddess appeared before me with tendrils that twisted down her back like vines. She was on her knees with her legs spread apart, pleasuring herself with nimble fingers. Greedily, her tongue lathered the shaft of my dick. I looked down in search of a thick coating of saliva, but only golden syrup dripped from her lips. It made me want her more. I noticed the same ambrosia running down either of her legs, pooling on the floor. She took note of my interest, stood up, and walked behind me.

Her breasts rested on my back as she leaned down to untie me. I rubbed my sore wrists, and my mouth watered in anticipation as she lay down on the floor in front of me. Her secretions became a golden river that ran the length of the marble floor. It rushed over her entire body, and every now and then, I caught a glimpse of her dark, taut nipples below the currents. She opened her legs for me, and the river split apart—now, it ran on both sides of her. Her body quivered, openly vulnerable. I knelt down between her thighs and inserted two fingers inside of her molten pussy. Her moans sounded like keys on a piano.

I wanted to hear more—I wanted to hear an entire song. I took my other hand and thumbed her clit. Her ass lifted all the way off the floor until it seemed like she was floating. She rode my hand. I quickly removed my fingers from her throbbing pussy, and she whimpered for the return of my languid touch. I plunged my hand into my mouth and savored the rich taste of molasses. Before she had the chance to exhale, I hungered for it again. I ran the tip of my tongue from the bottom to the top of one of her pussy lips. I did the same to the other and teased her clit with my tongue in a rapid, circular motion.

Her body jerked when I wrapped my lips around the firm nub and sucked. I blew on her damp vulva and gave it a French kiss. Connie began to twitch uncontrollably. She came in my mouth until my teeth ached from the sweetness, and I dribbled down my chin. I gave her tiny pecks all the way up her body. I nibbled on one of her nipples while I massaged the other with my thumb and forefinger. I continued the trail with my lips until I found hers and slowly slipped my tongue inside her mouth. She kissed me back with fervor and explored every curve of my lips, loving the taste that belonged to her. I gripped her hair with one hand while I guided my dick inside of her with the other. I moaned when I felt the wet heat at the beginning of her canal. One inch. Two inches. Her pussy tightened around my dick as I filled her gently and deliberately. Connie's moans found a subtle harmony with my own. She opened her legs wider until she was doing a full split on her back. That drove me wild. I slipped my hands underneath her ass and did away with being gentle. I began to pound her pussy until my balls slapped against her ass cheeks. Connie's screams brought me to another place.

$$$$

I was back in my room in my parent's New Jersey apartment. The muffled noises had awakened me. I was a nine-year-old kid in blue pajamas with little footballs covering them. I wiped the crust out of my eyes and climbed out of bed—I had peed through my sheets again, and my dad was going to be mad. I quietly tiptoed down the hall as the noises grew louder. My parent's door was slightly ajar, and I could see my mother on all fours while my dad hovered over her backside. They were both naked. I had overheard some of the kids at school talking about "doing it," but that was the only time I had caught my parents. My mother was crying, and I wasn't sure if he was supposed to be hurting her.

"You can't fuck no more either?" he snarled, and pushed her aside.

The room reeked of alcohol. My mom fell on her face, and her sobs deepened. "I'm trying, Tommy—it s . . . seems like I can't do anything to . . . to please you!"

"Are you saying this is my fault? Well, it's not my fault you can't fuck, you fucking prude! All you wanna do is lie on your back like a dead body! Do I need to find another broad that'll let me stick it up her ass?"

"You bastard!" she shouted, and began to pound on his chest. My dad shoved her back down and slapped her across the face. He held her down on the bed by the neck and slapped her relentlessly until I thought her head would fly off. My feet were glued to the carpet.

"Don't you ever fucking touch me, bitch!" He began to shake her instead. "I'm gonna teach you to respect me!" He pulled her off the bed by her hair, and her body slammed against the floor with a nauseating thud. Dad rummaged through one of his drawers like a mad man and threw inanimate objects across the room. When he found the belt he was looking for, he snapped it tautly between his hands and turned to face her. The belt buckle glinted in the light that came through the blinds. He looped the belt, held it above his head, and brought it down across her naked shins. Ma screamed and dragged herself across the coarse carpet to escape him. He moved towards her and struck her again. He continued to hit her until welts formed along her legs, and they began to bleed. Dad threw the belt down on the floor and grabbed a wine bottle off the nightstand.

He poured the alcohol into her bloody sores, and she squealed like she was dying. I covered my ears and backed away from the door. Tears ran down my face as I cowered in the hallway. I brought my knees to my chin and prayed to God that he would stop. The screams continued until I went deaf, and my ears began to ring.

$$$$

The screams were suddenly my own. I was conscious again, all thanks to my brief nightmare. I waited for the men to come back and kill me . . .

Chapter 1

I met Connie about a year ago. She didn't call herself Connie though, at least not in her trade of entertaining men. I was traveling down from Staten Island, New York, itching to open another restaurant that served fine Italian cuisine.

Business was booming at Balducci's, but I couldn't pass up the prospect of earning more money in Virginia Beach—the Southern resort area was a virtual goldmine. Who knew that when I got down there, I would not only be putting money into a second restaurant, but a woman's thong as well?

$$$$

As I cruised the interstate, I remembered that morning I was scheduled to leave, because I had been fucking Sylvia—she was like a cold fish beneath me, and it was the first time I had ever slapped the shit out of my wife. It wasn't that we weren't attracted to each other, because we both took special pains to look exactly the way we did eight years ago when I was twenty-eight and she was twenty-six—we did everything from exercising to receiving facials together. Sylvia's tummy was still as flat as any teenager's, and women would kill for her ample breasts and rounded ass. Not to mention the onyx hair that cascaded down her back for days.

My Mediterranean looks complemented her own—in the past, she could never keep her hands out of my shoulder-length, brownish hair or snatch herself away from my hazel eyes which had captivated her in the first place. I refused to look like the typical, spiky-haired, young punks on Staten Island. I had become a successful restaurateur when I made the transition from chef to owner—I took away most of the loyal patrons at the popular venue up the block I had sliced and diced for when those customers realized my cooking was going elsewhere.

Eventually, the place went out of business; the owner, Larry Pantone, went so far as to harass me at my then new establishment and make threatening phone calls to my home. The chaos ended not to long after that when the police escorted him out of Balducci's. I had never liked the greedy asshole anyway. But getting back to my dry, Saharan dick—I estimated two years of sexual tension, because the warmth in Sylvia's feline eyes disappeared shortly after the birth of Balducci's. She thought she wasn't number one anymore. The arguments had followed and then the short-lived, listless sex. I made the decision to name my second restaurant Venice, the city of my wedding proposal. I thought it would please her, but it didn't. She continued to stifle the intimacy I craved to punish me for my supposed lack of attention.

How many times did I have to convince her that we lived this way because of all my hard work? She didn't have to lift one damned, manicured finger. It was this thought that made me thrust into her with wild abandonment and anger to get some sort of reaction. Her vaginal muscles contracted and the left corner of her mouth twitched—I knew my wife's body, and there was no question in my mind that she wanted to succumb to my dick but was fighting the urge. My hair fell into my face like a psycho. I wanted to see her face twist in ecstasy, to feel the lock of her legs around my waist while she moaned my name like she used to. Yet, she pursed her lips even tighter, and when she rolled her eyes, I came inside of her from sheer frustration.

"Fuck!" I shouted.

"Wish you could," she muttered, flipping that luscious mane of silk over one shoulder. Her red talons clutched a Marlboro on the nightstand, and she lit it despite the tremors that pulsed through her fingers. She knew that a comment like that one could get her the silent treatment for a week, because that was how I dealt with my short temperament lately. I couldn't revert back to my old ways.

When we first got together, Sylvia discovered the anger management classes I was forced to attend. After watching my drunken father beat the shit out of my mother on countless days and blacken a cashier's eye for saying "hello" to Mom the wrong way, it was no wonder my temper had been maniacal. I guess smashing a guy's Cadillac windshield, after he cut me off, with the bat in my trunk was enough for the judge to say, "You can pay a fine and go to jail, or you can take the classes." Road rage is a bitch.

Nonetheless, Sylvia, a paralegal at the time exiting the same courtroom I was sentenced in, was drawn to my chivalry and witty nature.

Or at least that's the lie she told me for fear that if she admitted she simply wanted to fuck me, I would call her a slut. I told her about my childhood. She didn't run away, like some of my ex-girlfriends, thinking I would turn out like my father. Anyway, I had never laid my hands on a woman. Okay, maybe I had shaken one or two, but I never hit them. Sylvia was a strong woman—a borderline bitch that could handle my temper— and I guess that's what made me fall in love with her.

$$$$

Of course that morning I didn't really like her, so I ignored her comment and swung my legs over the side of the bed to slip on my cotton briefs. "I'm leaving for two months, and this is how you act?" I asked.

"You shouldn't be leaving at all. Not for two damned months anyway. How did you expect me to react?"

"I don't know how many times I have to explain to you that this isn't a vacation. It's a business trip that could benefit the both of us."

"Well, I'm tired of sitting in this house all day. I want to go back to work, Chris—I don't know why I let you talk me into leaving."

I sighed impatiently.

"I thought we agreed that you didn't have to work anymore after my business took off."

"No, you agreed. And I'm really getting sick and tired of you trying to control me all of a sudden."

"Control you? Is it such a big deal that I don't think my wife should have to work? You should be grateful."

"Well, I can make my own decisions, thank you. I'm not your mother." My eyes turned into dangerous little slits, and I moved so close to her that I could hear her heart beating.

"What did you say?"

"I said I'm not—" Before the last words could escape from her mouth, I knocked the spit out of it. I drew back my burning hand, and Sylvia looked at me in disbelief with a red handprint on her cheek. Even though she had pissed me off, I couldn't believe I had slapped her. I was instantly ashamed, and I turned away from her so that I could go to the bathroom where I wouldn't have to face her.

All of a sudden, a sensational pain went up my spine. I spun around, and Sylvia was naked on her hands and knees, panting like a dog in heat on our bed. The fury burned in her face, mirroring the cigarette that dangled from her pouty lips. I glanced towards the bathroom door and noticed the small, heart-shaped, fifteen-hundred dollar vase I had bought her on our third anniversary still rolling across the carpet. Sylvia gnashed her teeth, a sign that she was ready for war.

"The next time you decide to put your motherfucking hands on me, you had better learn how to sleep with both eyes open!" She stubbed out the flimsy cigarette in her crystal ashtray. Thank God, she didn't hurl that at me. "You think I don't get a little upset that the only time you decide to fuck me is right before you make your business trips?"

She had every right to be angry with me after what I had done, but I, too, was angry with her for disrespecting my dead mother the way she had. I could see in her eyes that she might try to hit me again, but we were both seething and probably would have went at it the second time around. I walked away instead.

Chapter 2

As though to clear my thoughts of what had happened that morning, I lowered my window and let the fresh air blow them away. The iridescent blue of my car gleamed in the sunlight as I headed down 264 East. I was only about thirty minutes away from the North End of Virginia Beach; I hoped that my cousin remembered to leave the key to his three-story condo under the doormat as promised.

Vince was a lot like me. He had built his own architectural firm from nothing; I fully respected him since we were both hotheads from the same seedy neighborhood and could have landed in jail during our youth. He had designed Balducci's as well as my new restaurant. When I pulled into the ritzy oceanfront suburb where he lived, I noticed a new bronze car made just like mine resting beside its red twin in his driveway. I was pleasantly surprised that he was home, and I looked at the bronze car in admiration.

Two luxury vehicles? Vince was definitely doing big things.

I hoisted my bags to the front door, glad to find it unlocked. I was just about to call out to Vince when I heard a door slam upstairs. A caramel-colored woman came careening downstairs. Her fuchsia lipstick was smeared, and her face was scrunched up like a slinky. Her breasts nearly popped out of her tube dress as she rudely brushed past me. Vince appeared at the top of the stairs and she made her way through the front door. There was a sly smile dancing across his face.

"What's the popular saying? You can't turn a hoe into a housewife?" he called out to her. The woman didn't even turn around and slammed the door behind her. I chuckled and set my bags on the floor.

"I see you haven't lost your touch, cousin." Vince walked down the steps and gave me a hug.

"Did you even have to wonder, Chris?" Every time I saw Vince, he was with some new broad. One couldn't truly respect any of the women Vince dated if they knew Vince. He had a way of finding some of the most beautiful and easy girls unlike any playboy I'd ever seen. It couldn't be because of his good looks—his elfin features reminded me of the Lucky Charm's leprechaun. He had tight hazel eyes like my own but small pointed ears and teeth. His head just reached the shoulders of my 6'1 frame. I figured it had something to do with the money Vince had no problem shedding to his advantage. His problem was he believed that his money, like most of the wealthy, made him invincible. I was poor once, so I never forgot where I came from. Vince, on the other hand, refused to remember.

"So, who was that one?" I asked him, plopping down on his ivory leather couch. Vince headed towards his eat-in kitchen to pop open a bottle of Merlot—I never did figure out how he could drink so early in the day. He lifted the glass to his lips, and the sly smile returned.

"Candy. And she tasted just like." He shook his head as though thinking of something funny. "Do you know this broad had the nerve to ask me if she could move in, just because she thought the pussy was that good?"

"And let me guess . . . you said, 'hell no,' she slapped you, since she gave up the ass, and then she walked out?"

"I might have considered it if I hadn't caught her talking to a friend on my phone about how she screwed me righteously and was set until the next tax season. They're all the same, these fucking broads." I walked into the kitchen and grabbed myself a glass, deciding to share a drink with my cousin for once. I inherited my father's temper, not his passion for alcohol.

"What did you expect, Vince? You know how you like 'em."

"Yeah, Chris, but I thought this one was different. She didn't ask to borrow my car until at least a month had passed so that she could brag to all her friends—I guess the titty bar where I met her should have tipped me off." I laughed so hard I nearly spit out the wine.

Chapter 3

That evening, Vince and I headed to downtown Virginia Beach to check out the building I hadn't seen in weeks—it was in a prime location since the city was turning the area into a mini-New York City with corporate towers, a new performing arts center, and a Central Park Drive to top it all off. Venice was finally complete. My cousin had talked it up as though it was some kind of dream. I didn't doubt that, because Vince was an artist when it came to his designs. I had given him full control over Venice because of his expertise.

I was certainly enticed as it loomed before me—it was a cream marble edifice with two pillars on each side of the entrance. The structure of my new restaurant reminded me of the summer night I had proposed to Sylvia, and then we made love like never before. I wanted my customers to have the same feeling when they tasted my food—like they were experiencing the best orgasm of their lives.

"You have outdone yourself, Vince," I whispered and let out a slow whistle. "I wish Sylvia could see this. She might stop being such a pain in the ass and realize how much money I could make down here."

"Don't worry, Chris," he responded. "I figured you were a little upset when I spoke to you this morning, since Sylvia's been keeping her legs shut, so I had plans for you to relax this evening." I wondered what Vince was up to now—for my cousin to be such a brilliant entrepreneur, he sure could tick me off with his wild antics sometimes, and I believed that he lived to get into trouble. With his hand still on my shoulder, Vince led me to his car.

"There's a black, titty bar down at the beach that—" I held my hand up to stop him.

"Hell no, Vince. I didn't come down here for that."

"Oh, give me a fucking break—you were the one who called me on the way here complaining about how Sylvia was giving you such a hard time. I thought maybe you could unwind while you took care of your business. You need to rest sometimes, Chris."

"I'll rest when I die. I didn't make it to where I am today by resting." Vince's face suddenly went solemn then he burst out laughing. I couldn't help but join in with him. My cousin always had that effect on me. Even when we were kids, he wanted to make the best out of any situation. "What's so damned funny?"

"Don't be such a drama king, Chris. Just come to the damned club."

"Drama king?" I said, trying to change the subject. "Is that one of the new terms from the Giordano dictionary, cuz it damned sure ain't Websters." Too bad Vince wasn't buying it. He could be as persuasive as a car salesman, and I finally gave in. Besides, a little female attention couldn't hurt, could it? It was something I certainly missed.

$$$$

When we stepped into the black gentlemen's club, I was more than a little nervous about Vince and I being the only two white patrons besides a white-haired man who looked to be someone's grandfather . . . or great-grandfather. Don't get me wrong, I'm no bitch, and the street I grew up on was predominantly black. But we were in a whole different neighborhood, and no matter whom I was cool with in Camden, it didn't count for shit here. It was pleasantly classy enough, though I shouldn't have been shocked given Vince's taste. No one seemed to pay us any mind.

The entire room, from the ceilings to the love seats aligning the mirrored walls, was drenched in maroon velvet. The name of the place was Addiction, and as soon as we took our seats at a table center-stage, I could see why. I looked up to see toffee and dark chocolate thighs contorting themselves into pretzels on the pole.

I had never been with a black woman, but it wasn't out of the question. I quickly shook my head, dismissing the lusty, curious thought—it would be incredibly easy here according to Vince, but I still loved Sylvia, and I hadn't cheated since we were two weeks into dating. I had barely sat down before the disc jockey called out a name that nearly knocked me off of my stool. Candy.

Sure enough, the same woman that had brushed past me like a hurricane this morning in Vince's condo sauntered down the catwalk. I glanced at Vince who didn't appear at all surprised. In fact, he was smirking. He knew she danced here.

"What the hell are you doing?" I hissed at him. "That broad was furious when she left your house this afternoon. You humiliate her then bring us to the titty bar where she works? What if she gets our asses kicked or something?" Vince waved his stubby hand as though I was a bothersome fly.

"She won't do that, Chris."

"Oh, yeah? You know something I don't?" Vince took a long swig of the apple martini a g-string clad waitress brought to our table.

"You think me calling her a whore was a figure of speech? We screw from time to time, and I pay her for it. Well." Apparently, I didn't know how badly my cousin's sexual habits were getting out of hand. I couldn't do anything but stare at him incredulously.

"She just got a little too comfortable, and I had to remind her where she stood.

Believe me, she loves the money more than her pride." I wrinkled my nose in half-mock, half-real disgust.

"I can't believe you paid for the ass." Vince winked at me.

"It was well worth it." As though she knew we were talking about her, Candy gyrated towards the end of the stage where we sat. I would have never guessed she was a dancer, let alone a prostitute—her baby face hid all traces of innocence lost. As she moved closer, I realized that she was actually quite beautiful. Her thick ruby lips spoke without opening, and her sleepy eyes were two searing pools of coffee. High cheek bones accentuated an otherwise heart-shaped face, and I was sure that she looked even better without the blonde bob atop her head. Sylvia's breasts were fuller than Candy's, but Candy's ass and thighs rumbled with thunder each time she took a step.

What the hell was I doing comparing the two? My wife and my cousin's whore? I just knew that Candy was going to proposition Vince, since he was already one of her clients, yet when she crooked her index finger at me, my mouth went dry.

She knelt down to my eye level, and I leaned in to find out what she could possibly want from me and not him.

"Would you like a dance?" Now, she was so close that her peppermint breath tickled my eyelashes. "Perhaps more?"

I watched Vince warily from the corner of my eye. He appeared to be quite amused by the spectacle in front of him. Maybe she thought it was that type of party because of who I had arrived with, but I wasn't willing to pay for sex. Ever. Sylvia and I may have been on thin ice, but we fucked for free. The dance, however, was still up for consideration. I rested my forearms beneath her and replied coolly,

"The dance is fine. More is out of the question." Candy gave me a sideways smile and extended her hand so that I could help her down. Her French-manicured nails dug softly into my palm as she walked me over to a separate room, and I briefly wondered what they would feel like on my back. I took one last look back at Vince to see if he was upset with how Candy had blatantly dismissed him, but he was already flirting with some Amazon beauty. I guess he knew Candy would come around sooner or later. A massive bouncer guarded the room we entered, and he gave me the once over with a scarred eye to conclude that I didn't pose a threat. The couches were white in that room and the black lights played across them, giving everything an alien glow. I fell back onto one of the couches, realizing how exhausted I was at that moment and how much Candy might relax me.

Without missing a beat, Candy slipped a hand behind her back to undo her red bikini top. It was as familiar to her as riding a bike.

Her perky breasts didn't spill out, because they sat just right. One thing that I did like about Candy from the start was her aggression, something I admired in any woman. She sat in my lap and began to grind as though that was all she had been thinking about up on that stage. The very thought that she desired me rather than it being the other way around was enough to send a hard-on right through my cream, linen pants. Candy giggled and turned around to straddle me.

"Someone's excited," she crooned.

"Naturally."

Her nipples tickled my chest, and she entwined her fingers in my hair.

It felt good when she did that. Apparently, my goatee wasn't bothering her soft skin, because she quickly buried her breasts in my face. Candy leaned back to get a good look at me.

I gave her a sideways smile.

"What?"

"You actually are quite fine, but then again, I'm sure you know that?"

If not for my olive complexion, I probably would have turned a bright red. My antsy fingertips lay at either side of me. I knew I wasn't allowed to touch her in there—shouldn't anyway. Instead, I replied, "You get paid to say shit like that, sweetheart." Candy prepared to bring that musical voice to my earlobe. She paused dramatically.

"This time, I mean it." With that, she flicked her tongue at my ear as any snake in the grass would do. I didn't move, didn't even breath for a moment. Her mouth suckled my neck as she went to work massaging my tense thighs and then sought out her final destination. I released a soft moan as Candy groped my dick, hating the fact that she had quickly gained the control but loving it all at the same time. She expertly unzipped my pants, and the friction of her hand against me was enough to send me over the edge right then and there. Shit, who could blame me? It had been a long time since I had someone all over me. Damn right, I could have been a minuteman from just one hand job.

As Candy jerked me off, I threw my head back and was forced to contain myself— I didn't forget about that giant at the door. Since I wasn't going to do it myself, Candy brought one of my hands to her breasts, and my first reaction was to tweak her nipples. This time, she let out a small sigh of satisfaction and enveloped the fingers I had touched her with inside of that pretty mouth.

Candy sucked on them like a newborn, and I wondered how that mouth would feel elsewhere. At first, I was intimidated by that brave act of hers, but suddenly, I changed my mind and tried to play catch up. I brought my other hand to the valley between her breasts and dragged my fingertips down past her belly button to the heat that rose in between her legs. I imagined the ambrosia and honey that would spill out if I gave her bikini bottom one slight—

A jerky motion near the doorway caused me to sit up straight. I couldn't tell if it was the sight of the bouncer pounding his meaty fists into the back of some poor soul's head that brought me back to my senses or a little voice in the back of mine. After mulling it over for a short period, I thanked God for the bouncer. Sylvia. Married. Candy. Vince's whore. All of these words came to mind in a soft chant as I remembered one of the fingers she sucked on bore a wedding ring. I flung Candy off of me and onto the other side of the couch. Her mouth opened into a silent "o" of surprise. I stood up and fumbled with the zipper on my pants.

"What the fuck are you trying to pull?" Candy crossed her arms across her chest defensively.

"I know you are not even trying to play like you didn't like that."

I acted as though I was engrossed with my zipper, so I wouldn't have to look at her. The sight of her statuesque body was still turning me on. "You fools are sooo fucking predictable. You weren't complaining when I was giving your dick a rub down. Now, the poor baby's feeling guilty cuz he's thinking about his wife at home," she finished in an infantile voice.

"Shutup."

"Why, because I'm right? If you hadn't seen Rodney whupping somebody's ass over there, you would have been all up in this pussy."

I spun around to see what had caught my attention a couple of seconds ago. I could hear a loud ruckus over the rhythm and blues that belted out of the speakers. I dashed to the door, leaving Candy behind, to find what could only be described as a bar fight inside of the club.

Vince was right in the middle of it, huddled in the fetal position on the floor—a bald-headed man continuously drove his foot into Vince's ribs, and it was all Vince's drunk ass could do to defend himself. The Amazon beauty tugged on Baldy's arm, but he ripped it away and sent her flying like a rag doll. Some of the other dancers shrieked in anger as their friend toppled to the floor. I could see one of the bouncers trying to get through the throng of people to come to Vince's defense, but I was closer to the brawl.

My first instinct was to grab a lone Heineken bottle off of a nearby table, and I did. I broke into a short sprint and lunged through the crowd, suit and all. The bottle smashed against the back of Baldy's head with a sickening crack, and he fell to his knees. It wasn't easy to grab Vince up off the floor with quivering hands, but I did. I pushed and elbowed our way through the flying fists. We bolted through the front door and never looked back.

Chapter 4

I lit into Vince after he told me how everything went down—apparently, that was the Amazon beauty's hubby coming to pick her up from an occupation he didn't even know she held. Vince was so inebriated and taken with Baldy's wife that he asked Baldy how much it would be for one night with her. I told Vince that he wasn't starring in Indecent Proposal, he was certainly no Robert Redford, and money cannot buy everything—especially from a very angry, possessive man. Vince eventually passed out in the backseat.

Somehow, he still managed to get up in the morning to meet with a pastor about designing a church. *How ironic*, I thought. *A sinner working for a saint.*

$$$$

Venice was even better during the day than it was at night. As I moved towards the kitchen, I took note of its attributes. There were Cathedral ceilings in the dining area and pillars throughout. The floors were a black marble, and there were wall-length, fish tanks ready to be brought to life. The kitchen was larger than the one in Balducci's, and I couldn't wait to start looking for a talented chef. I heard a slight noise behind me and went back into the dining area to find out what it was.

Candy leaned against one of the pillars like she was waiting for me. Her white sundress clung to her shapely hips and thighs, and the blonde wig was gone. Her real, auburn-colored hair billowed down her shoulders. She looked fabulous, but I didn't want my cousin's whore anywhere near me. Suppose one of her gentlemen callers came after me like Baldy came after Vince?

"What the hell are you doing here?"

"I wanted to apologize about what I said last night." I couldn't understand why, seeing as how we barely knew each other. I noticed that she didn't walk like she was onstage anymore. If anything, she seemed very vulnerable and afraid. A completely different person. But I was not the one to be fooled so easily when possums played dead.

"Apologize for what, Candy?"

"My name is Constance," she murmured.

"What?"

"I said my name is Constance." What an old name for such a young girl, or at least Constance looked younger at that very moment with so little makeup on. I felt a slight twinge of guilt for letting someone who looked no older than twenty-three ravage my thirty-six-year-old body. "And I was talking about the smart-ass comment I made about your wife." I eyed her suspiciously.

"You came all the way over here to tell me that? And how did you know where I was anyway?" Constance toyed with the flap on the straw clutch she carried.

"I was coming over to pay Vince a visit when I saw you two leaving the condo. So, I followed you from there."

"Well, you found me. Apology accepted. You can see yourself out." I made my way back towards the kitchen and Constance followed me, gently grabbing my elbow. Why didn't she just give it up?

"I thought maybe we could do lunch, so I could make it up to you." She was playing games again. She was a prostitute, and that's what they did. I guessed since Vince had discarded her, she had set her eyes on me.

Maybe she had smelled the Armani linen on my back. But I wasn't Vince, and she wasn't reeling me in.

"Not a good idea, Constance. No offense, but my cousin told me about your, um, arrangement. Personally, I'm not interested."

"That's not why I'm here. I was talking out of my ass last night. I heard about your situation with your wife, and I never should have said those nasty things to you."

"What the hell did Vince tell you?" I asked angrily. How dare he talk about my personal life with some stranger, a hooker no less?

"It wasn't Vince's fault. He had you on speakerphone when you called him on your way to Virginia and—"

"Wait a minute. He had me on speakerphone?" She looked away.

"We were, uh, preoccupied when you called, and he didn't pick it up." Constance grabbed my hand, and I was terribly uncomfortable with the way she looked at me. I was even more uncomfortable with the fact that she knew my business. "Look, I know what it's like to be rejected by someone you love. Especially when you think you're doing all the right things.

I know you're not an asshole, because if you were, things could have gone even further last night despite what went down at the bar. We were tucked away in a separate room . . ."

I swallowed the lump in my throat.

"I'm not going to discuss my marriage with you."

"That's fine. We can still have lunch on me."

I wasn't sure that I trusted her intentions, but her apology seemed sincere. What the hell, I was starving.

Chapter 5

Constance took me to an old-fashioned drive-in called Doumar's in Norfolk. I appreciated the Southern hospitality of my teenaged servers. I watched in amazement as Constance wolfed down a large cheeseburger and fries, already knowing where it all went. She washed it down with one of the best vanilla shakes I had ever tasted.

Constance began rambling on about the classes she was taking up at a local community college. She told me that she wanted to become an accountant despite certain hurdles in her life that interrupted her education. She gave me an inquisitive look.

"What? You don't think I have goals because I strip?" I looked out the passenger-side window of her '98 Camaro. I couldn't say a damned thing, because she was right. "I can only imagine the shit Vince has been talking."

"Well, it's kinda hard not to believe. Especially after what happened last night.

You came on very strong, and you don't even know me."

She smiled sheepishly.

"You didn't try to stop me."

"It can never happen again, Connie."

Her eyes appeared to warm.

"My big brother was the first to call me that—he thought Constance was too grown up."

"Does he call you Constance now because you're a little older—how old are you anyway?"

"I'm twenty-four and . . . and he's dead." Connie's words caught in her throat, but she quickly regained her composure. I hardly wanted her to get emotional with me, so I switched the conversation back to what happened the night before.

"Connie?" Her eyes snapped back to me as though she had forgotten I was sitting right next to her. "Let's just forget about what happened in that room, okay? I'm married, and it never should've gone that far to begin with. I don't want Vince's seconds, and I don't agree with your profession. I mean dancing is one thing—"

“Look, Vince is the only person who is paying me to sleep with him.” I raised an eyebrow, and she gave me an “are you calling me a liar” look. “Seriously, I really need the money, but I’m too scared to do that kind of thing with too many people. Vince is my first and only client. I guess I came on to you because he made me mad. He never made me feel like a whore until yesterday when he called me one.”

“If you really need the money, just get another job like the rest of us. Then you won’t have to deal with the bullshit.”

“It’s not that simple, Chris. I’ve got school and—” She bit her lip. “You wouldn’t understand.” We were quiet for a moment. It was all getting too serious for me, so I suggested that we head back.

$$$$

I had already learned more about Connie than I really wanted, and I wondered why I had accepted her invitation when I could’ve gotten something to eat alone. I didn’t think about it too long, because I noticed something different about my Mercedes as we turned into the restaurant's parking lot—someone had keyed it so badly that the scratches looked like the lines on the inside of my hand. I jumped out of Connie's car, and my eyes dashed left to right as though I was looking at a tennis match. Someone had scratched up my car. My first prized possession. "Oh shit, Chris," Connie said softly, bringing a hand to her mouth. "Call the police."

"And tell them what, Connie?" I barked. There was a possibility that the vandal could be a jealous stalker of hers. I was too mad to think.

"I am so sorry, Chris. Maybe we shouldn't have—"

"Yeah, maybe we shouldn't have. Let's go. I'm getting fucking pissed off just standing here." Something stopped me though—I saw a black car parked at a weird angle in front of the shopping complex across the street.

The driver began to creep along with the laziness of someone wanting to be noticed. I craned my neck to get a better look at the make and model of the vehicle. Without warning, the black car sped off into the sea of traffic along the boulevard. The driver weaseled his way in between two compact cars and disappeared.

Chapter 6

The more I thought of some idiot scratching my shit up, the more my fury rose. I wished I had a punching bag in front of me like the one I kept in my basement. Or better yet, the idiot himself.

Vince was downstairs with a bunch of bags from Macys surrounding him. He frowned when he saw the look on my face. I slammed the door behind me.

"What's going on, Chris? You look like you could kill somebody." I immediately went for a glass of Merlot. "And you're drinking?"

"Some asshole keyed my car."

"What?"

"Yeah, you heard me right."

"When the hell did this happen?"

"I was coming from . . . out of the restaurant to get something from my car, and the shit was scratched up."

"Did you see anything or call the police?"

"No. I wish I had caught the prick. And who I really gotta call is Sylvia. I didn't even let her know I made it here safely. Maybe she can help me calm down." Vince shook his head sympathetically and peered out the bay window to look at my car. "Fuck! I'm sorry it had to happen here, Chris."

"Well, I had to come down here on business. It was probably just some stupid kids." I tried to convince myself of that ever since I had left Connie standing in the parking lot. "I'll have to get a paint job while I'm down here."

"I know a guy that does a damned good job. I'm just surprised that you're handling this so well."

"I guess anger management taught me something," I said with a wry smile. "So, where are you headed? I know you only shop like this when you're getting ready to go out of town."

"I got business to take care of in New York. Some rich bitch that was visiting down here for the weekend happens to be the sister of one of my old clients. She was so impressed with her sister's home that she wants me to design something for her too."

"Well, at least one of us is in a good mood. How long will you be gone?"

"About two weeks."

"You'll be coming back when I'm leaving."

"Why, you gonna miss me?" he mocked.

"Hardly."

"Make yourself at home while I'm gone. I'm catching a cab to Norfolk International at eight, and my flight leaves at ten. I think I'll take a nap until then."

Once Vince headed upstairs to finish packing and catch some rest, I picked up the phone to give Sylvia a ring. Her mother, Elaine, answered the phone. As usual, her voice was cool and detached.

I couldn't stand the snobbish bitch—she thought I was beneath her just because I grew up in Camden, New Jersey. It didn't matter that I owned a restaurant. It didn't matter that I lived in one of the swankiest neighborhoods in Staten Island, because I didn't come from money. But I knew that money couldn't cure or cover up everything—Elaine was bipolar, and her rich husband didn't want his circle of friends to find out about her crazy mood swings. "Christopher, what a pleasant surprise." I even hated the way she said my name.

"It's a surprise that I'm calling my own house?"

"No. I simply thought that you would be caught up in the little restaurant you're opening in Virginia." My grip tightened on the receiver. The *little* restaurant.

"Where's Sylvia?" There was a brief pause, and my wife came to the phone.

"Hey, baby." Her anger seemed to have sizzled down. "How's everything going? Is the place what you thought it would be?"

"It's beautiful, honey—look, I got some not so good news."

"What's wrong, Chris? Don't tell me you have to stay even longer."

"No, nothing like that. My car got vandalized." There was a short moment of silence, and I waited for her soothing voice to return. Fuck soothing.

"Where and when the hell did this happen? I thought Vince lived in a good neighborhood!"

"It got keyed sometime this afternoon in front of the restaurant. I went to check the place out, and when I came back outside, it was all messed up. Why are you yelling at me?"

"I had a bad feeling about this trip to begin with. If you hadn't gone down there, this wouldn't have happened! I don't even know if running a business down there is such a smart idea—you don't know anything about the area, and it's a big-ass risk. That was just the first sign."

I couldn't believe she was acting like I asked for it.

"Give it a damned rest, okay? Sometimes, you have to take risks in life to get ahead. And I didn't call you to argue. I'm already pissed off, so don't start this shit now."

"I'm not starting anything. I'm looking out for your best interests."

"The hell you are. You're looking out for yours. You know if I make this step, it's going to be a lot more responsibility for me. But I also know it's going be a lot more success for the both of us."

"Less time for the both of us too." I sighed.

"Sylvia, if you could just give me a little time and some patience—hopefully, we'll be able to retire early and spend each moment together."

"Well, I'm not willing to wait forever."

"What's that supposed to mean? It's either you or my career? You can be so damned self-centered sometimes."

"I can afford to be. I helped you finance Balducci's. If it wasn't for me, you wouldn't be where you are today."

"I paid back every penny like I said I would. I didn't ask you for a damned dime anyway. I was willing to do whatever it took to get that restaurant—I can't believe you just said that to me!"

"And I can't believe that you can make time for everything else but not your marriage."

The conversation was going nowhere and everywhere I didn't want it to. I tried to soften my tone.

"Vee, I hope that one day you realize how much I love you. I hope you realize you were the reason I was brave enough to open up a restaurant . . . I don't see that same encouragement now."

"Success is knowing when you've gained enough of it. You love me, and you love your work, Chris. The question is, which one do you love more?" She quietly hung up the phone.

Chapter 7

I must have fallen asleep on Vince's couch. I saw a note on the end table with Vince's scribbled handwriting telling me that he had left. I went into the kitchen and was happy to see that he had enough ingredients for me to make my famous pollo al forno—Vince liked to cook too, but he wasn't as good as me.

While my dinner cooked, I flipped through the channels on the television but stopped to look at a story on the evening news—there had been a rash of car vandalisms at various shopping complexes in Virginia Beach and Chesapeake. Apparently, they were related to gang initiations. The thought occurred to me that I may have been a victim. Maybe Connie wasn't to blame.

The phone rang and I picked it up, thinking that it might be Vince calling to see if I was still pissed. It was Connie.

"Hey. You looking for Vince?"

"I called for you, actually." Thank God, Vince wasn't home. I didn't want him to think I was a womanizer too.

"I don't think it was a good idea for you to call me here, Connie."

"Well, I didn't have any other way to contact you, and I wanted to make sure you were alright after what happened today." I finally smiled for the first time in a couple of hours.

"I'm hanging in there. Trying not to let myself get too upset."

"Would you like some company?"

"Are you crazy? Vince is here," I lied. There was no way I was letting Connie come over here when it would just be the two of us. Who knew what could happen.

"No, he's not Chris. He tried to get with me before he went to New York tonight—he had some damned nerve, too, after the way he spoke to me."

I got caught in that one. Since I couldn't think of any other reason for her not to come over, I just gave it to her straight.

"Connie, look . . . I am attracted to you, that's no surprise. So I don't think it would be a good idea for you to come over here tonight." Connie giggled.

"I don't know if I should be disappointed or flattered. But I wasn't going to try anything. I just enjoy good conversation, and I'm not working at the club tonight."

"Still, Connie—"

"Okay, I won't push. I'm glad you're better. You have a good night, Chris."

"Goodnight."

I went out onto the balcony, lit a cigar, and leaned back on the chaise lounge. My mind skipped over the events of the day. Maybe I should call Connie back, I thought. I was stressing, and I needed to talk to somebody. Sylvia was definitely out of the question, and I didn't keep a lot of friends.

I was cooking way too much food for just myself—no, it wouldn't be very bright to offer Connie an invitation. I thought it over a few more times then found myself pressing the caller i.d. button on the phone. Gary Walker was the name that popped up. Did she live with a man? A boyfriend maybe? Why did I even care? I figured if she had called me a few minutes ago then he couldn't be there with her. I dialed the number back. Connie picked up after the first ring. "Chris?"

"Yeah, are you hungry?"

$$$$

I knew it wasn't a good idea after I answered the door. Although Connie arrived wearing a white hooded pullover, loose-fitting jeans, and sneakers, I still thought she looked cute. And incredibly sexy. Her ponytail swung behind her as she took a seat at the dining room table like she probably had several times with Vince. I found it very ironic that she had attempted to dress a little less appealing but ended up turning me on even more. Her pants, although a little baggy, still clung to the right place.

"So, let's see how good you really are," she said, preparing to dig into the food I had set. "Damn, Chris. This is really good! Continue your day job."

"Thanks. I got plenty of practice way before Balducci's. I can't wait 'til my second restaurant opens."

"Me, either. I'll probably get as big as a house when it does."

"Then they'll have to roll you down the stage at Addiction. You might even knock the pole down." We both laughed. I cleared my throat, and since the mood was light, I casually asked, "How does Gary feel about you stripping?" Connie's full lips stretched into one thin line. I had the distinct feeling that I just put my foot in my mouth.

"You know Gary?" she spat out. Apparently, there was no love lost between the two.

"No, but—"

"Gary's my uncle, not my man." I looked down at my plate.

"I'm sorry for making assumptions. It's just that I saw the name on the caller—" Connie's entire demeanor had changed, so I dropped it. "How are your classes coming along?"

The ominous clouds in her eyes passed.

"I'm getting A's in all of them."

"Keep up the good work." We finished our meal, and I cleaned up the kitchen while Connie lay sprawled out on the ivory carpet by the fireplace. I brought Connie a second glass of wine, and we talked until the wee hours of the morning. We must have dozed off watching Bad Boys, because my cell phone began ringing at about two-thirty a.m. I knew by the ring tone that it was Sylvia, and I glanced at Connie with a twinge of guilt—I decided I wasn't going to answer the phone. Even though Connie was curled up asleep on the floor, I didn't want to get into it with my wife. I placed the phone on vibrate after it stopped ringing and lay my head on the chair arm. Connie began to stir. She glanced up at me with sleepy eyes.

"What time is it?" she asked.

"Three a.m." Those two eyes widened.

Connie quickly rose to her feet and headed for the front door.

"I have to get out of here."

She burst through the door and jogged down the driveway. I couldn't help but wonder why she was in such a hurry.

"Thanks for the dinner, Chris," she yelled over her shoulder.

"No problem," I said as I watched her fumble with the keys to her car.

She got in safely, and I went back inside the condo to turn off the television. I noticed that Connie had left behind her wallet on the floor near the couch. I ran back outside with it and called out her name.

Connie had to have heard me, because she was still in the driveway with her windows down. She abruptly threw the car into reverse and dashed down the street.

I still couldn't figure out what that was all about, but I was tired as hell. Perhaps I was crazy too, because I felt as though someone lingered in the shadows, hiding behind the cars lining the quiet street. The stranger's eyes studied me. I couldn't see them, but I could feel them like a winter draft raking over my face.

A chill tickled the back of my neck, and I went into the house locking everything behind me.

Chapter 8

The next day, I decided to take some time out for myself, because I wasn't over the vandalism just yet. I called for a taxi to pick me up from the shop where I was having my car repainted. The driver took me to Avis to rent another vehicle. I could have taken one of Vince's cars, but I was wary about using either one of them since my own car had been vandalized.

I didn't need anything fancy, just something to get me from A to B. I settled for a 2007 Ford Focus. I headed to Addiction—it was the only place that would take away the tension headache pounding in my head like a prisoner's fists against metal bars. I didn't know if Connie would be there or not, but it was the first spot that came to mind and I hoped she was. I was glad that she had left her wallet at Vince's—I had an excuse to see her.

I knew it was dumb as hell to go back to the gentleman's club. Someone might recognize me as the bottle-toting fool from the previous night. Perhaps one of Baldy's friends. Hopefully, I was lucky and they hadn't gotten a good look at me during the ruckus. But then, I never did believe in luck.

Frantically, I searched for her when I stepped inside of Addiction. I wanted to sniff a line of her perfume and drink in every part of her body even if for a brief moment of tipsiness. I decided to take a seat at the bar so that I could scan the entire room, but Connie was nowhere to be found. I opened up the wallet and thought of the only other option—I could drop by her house. Of course, I had no idea what would be waiting for me there. Connie's personal life was still a mystery to me, because I didn't know too much about her outside of the club. And then there was this Gary person who was supposedly an uncle. There were no good reasons for me to pay her a visit.

Still, I opened the wallet with a cavalier flick of my wrist and saw Connie's smiling face looking up at me. It was corny, but I smiled back. The driver's license revealed her address in Norfolk, and I asked the bartender if she knew where it was.

She scribbled down the directions on a napkin, and I was out the door again.

$$$$

I pulled up to a red and white home in the Berkeley section of Norfolk. It was a beautiful Victorian. A porch wrapped itself around the house, resembling a woman clinging to her man. Someone had left an ash-tray on the porch's swing. I wondered who smoked, because I hadn't smelled cigarettes on Connie's breath. I looked at the napkin again to make sure the address was correct and rang the doorbell. I hoped someone answered quickly because there were three young black men eyeing me from the corner across the street, and I appeared to be unwelcome. I glared back at them. Much like today's youth—black, white, and otherwise—they didn't seem to have a problem with their jeans hanging off their asses, sweeping the sidewalk. The June heat sunk into my black Marc Jacobs shirt, and I prayed that someone would answer. Someone must have heard what I was thinking, because the lock turned and the door opened a crack.

"Yeah?" said the raspy voice with a strong Southern twang.

"I'm looking for Connie Green. Does she live here?"

"Who askin'?"

"My name is Chris. Chris Balducci. I'm a friend of hers. She left her wallet at my cousin's place last night." I held the Liz Claiborne wallet in the air to verify what I had just told him. As he opened the door a little wider, the voice behind the door became a visible figure. I recoiled in disgust. The man before me was stout and round in stature, vaguely reminding me of The Penguin from the Batman movie. His large eyes bulged out of their yellow sockets like a bug's. If he had a dick, it was hidden by the protruding belly underneath his soiled wifebeater.

"Sorry, Chris," he said, extending his hand. "I'm Connie's Uncle Gary. "You can neva be too sho 'bout who's comin' to yo' doe out here. But you shole don't sound like or look like you from 'round here anyways."

"I'm from Jersey."

"Mmm-hmm. Come on in 'fore them niggas cross the street try to start somethin' wit you."

"Well, I just came by to—"

"Boy, come on in here and get you a cool drink. It's hot as shit today." I gave up and followed the waddling man into the house. A stench hung in the air like ten-day-old milk and musty clothes. As I passed through the foyer to the kitchen, I realized that there were pictures of Connie hanging on all the walls. I saw Connie as a baby on a rocking horse, a toddler-sized Connie throwing her head back in laughter with her arm wrapped around a tree, Connie who looked to be about thirteen running around a track wearing a uniform, and a more recent unsmiling picture of Connie as a high school senior. That photograph held a sadness that gripped me. Something else that unsettled me was the fact that there were pictures of no one else anywhere—not Connie's parents, or her brother, or even Uncle Gary.

Gary poured me a glass of iced tea and leaned back on the countertop with his arms folded across his flabby chest. His eyes bore into me from across the room. I could have sliced the uncomfortable silence with a knife. He pulled one from a drawer and proceeded to cut up an apple. I was glad that he was focused on something else besides me.

"You new to Virginia?"

"Nope. I've been here a couple times. Down here on business right now."

"How did you meet my niece?" I swallowed hard. He watched my Adam's apple rise and fall.

"I told you, remember? She's a friend of my cousin I'm staying with."

"Who?"

"Carla," I lied.

Carla was the chef at my restaurant and her name was the first one to come to mind.

"They wait tables at the same place or somethin'?" I didn't know what the hell he was talking about, but I just went along with whatever lie Connie must have told him about her night job.

"Yeah, Carla's been there for a while."

He gnawed on the apple with the rotted yellow things in his mouth I guessed were his teeth.

"So," he started with a snide grin, "is you and Connie fuckin'?"

"What?" I sputtered, my mouth full of tea.

"Some pretty white boy comes into my house wit my niece's wallet. She must not have been thinkin' too clearly to leave her wallet behind. I gots to wonder if you doin' somethin' wit my baby girl."

"Connie and I are not sleeping together. We're just friends through my cousin like I said."

"Where you say she left the wallet?"

"At Carla's house."

"Why Carla ain't bring it then?"

"She had to work today."

I didn't appreciate the line of questions he asked, and I was under the distinct impression that this man was challenging me.

"Hmmph. I ain't neva met no Carla." I rose to thank the man for his nasty-ass tea and be on my way when I heard the front door close. Connie walked into the kitchen, and her accounting books fell to the filthy, tiled floor once she saw me.

Chapter 9

"**Chris," she said**, her voice strained. "What are you doing here?"

"You left your wallet at Carla's. You two must have been tired after waiting tables all night." Connie's eyes narrowed then widened once she realized the story I had fabricated.

"Oh, yeah." She chuckled nervously. "Thanks for bringing it over. Tell Carla I'll be seeing her later." Gary's eyes never wavered as he took in the exchange between the two of us. He knew she was lying.

"Constance, what you doin' home so damn late?" The harsh way he spoke to her caught me off guard.

"You know I got my classes today, Uncle Gary." Connie kneeled down to pick her books up, and her eyes remained at her feet.

"Hmmph. Classes ain't nothin' but a damn waste of time if you ask me. Told you I could git you a job at the shipyard wit me if you wanted it. Make you some real money. Guess that ain't good enough fo' yo' spoiled ass, is it?" Constance chewed on her bottom lip and said nothing. "Anyway, go run me my bath. It should be done time I get up there. You know it's hard for me to make it up them stairs with this bad hip."

It's probably hard for your fat ass to make it anywhere, I thought. "I'm goin' to Colonial Downs this weekend to play the horses. Git me some dough on the side. I want this house clean when I get back, ya hear?"

"Yes, sir." Connie sounded very down, and I wanted to punch him right in that thick gut. Belittling her like that in front of me and ordering her around like a maid! I could see why she rushed home the night before—she probably had a curfew too. Connie headed for the stairs to do as he requested but not before he caught her around the waist with his arm.

"You know I only want the best fo' you baby," he said, his tone much lighter. The hand that rested on her bare midriff slowly stroked the soft flesh there. It made me shiver. Connie forced a smile and nodded her head. She wouldn't look at me as she started up the stairs again.

Gary was so busy watching Connie that he didn't even notice when I left.

$$$$

The three young men were still standing on the corner when I came outside. My nosiness got the best of me, and I approached them. The boys stood up straighter to mark their territory and lifted their chins.

"What the hell you want, man?" the tallest one asked me.

He couldn't have been any more than seventeen or eighteen.

"What do you know about the girl that lives in that house I just came from?"

"You oughta know a lot since you just came outta there." The other two snickered. I pulled a twenty dollar bill out of my back pocket.

"What do you know now?"

"Wait a minute, you a cop, man?"

"No, just a concerned friend." He hesitated and snatched the money from my hand.

"What you wanna know exactly?" Why I wanted to know was the question. I guess that Gary character had really gotten to me. He acted like he was Connie's possessive boyfriend rather than her uncle.

"First off, who is that man she's living with?"

"Dude is her uncle." Okay, so that much was true. However, the fact that he was family angered me even more with him treating and touching her like that.

"How is their relationship? Bad or really bad?" The kid scratched the back of his tatooed neck like he didn't want to answer that question.

"Man, dude is a nasty ass old man. Always pattin' her ass when she leave or tryin' to kiss her neck. I be seein' him—I live two doors down and I caught him a few times real early in the mornin' on my way to the bus stop. I know wassup wit that."

"Well, where are her mother and father?" The kid and his two friends shook their heads.

"It was messed up, man. Her parents and her brother got killed right up the street on their way home from the store by a drunk driver, 'bout six or seven years ago. Then she came to live wit him. Shit, I was a shorty then. She was the only one who made it outta that car alive." I thanked the kid and walked over to my car. I didn't want Connie left alone in that house, but I was in no position to do anything for her. Maybe I would come up with something later to try and help her. I had just unlocked the car door before someone rammed my head into the roof of the Focus—my skull bounced against the hot metal and snapped backwards.

Chapter 10

I fell to my knees and placed my hands flat on the ground. I turned to face my attacker. Two very dark faces looked down at me menacingly. Two attackers.

"What the fuck—" was all I could manage before one picked me up by my collar and the other began pummeling my face. I could see the three teenagers out of the corner of my swelling eye running in the opposite direction. The tallest one glanced over his shoulder as though he felt sorry for me and kept moving.

"Hey, what yall doin' over there?" I heard a voice screech somewhere in the distance. The one who drove his knuckles into my face looked back, and I seized the opportunity. I threw my knee into his groin, and he doubled over in pain, letting out an agonizing groan. That startled the other one, and he lunged at me with his arms flailing. Realizing that he was indeed the weaker fighter, I blocked one of his punches with my left forearm and drove my right fist into his chin as hard as I could. He toppled backwards and hit the hard asphalt. *That's right motherfucker*, I thought, *you picked the wrong man to rob today*. I stomped on his chest to compensate for my aching forehead and finally got the car door unlocked. I'm not a bitch, but I'm not a dummy either—the two of them could have easily kicked my ass if they got up in time. I started up the car and dug my foot into the accelerator in one fluid movement. I sped through the narrow streets, trying to remember how to get to the interstate. I looked up into the rearview mirror and did a double take.

There was Baldy, right on my tail, in a green, 1978 Oldsmobile Cutlass Supreme. The sneering face that glared back at me suggested that he knew who I was and wanted to do me bodily harm.

He followed dangerously close to my bumper—about two feet away. I made a sharp left. I was glad when I saw the ramp that would take me back to 264 East. I weaved in and out of traffic, car horns blaring all around me, but I still couldn't shake the determined fucker. I didn't want him to find out where Vince lived so I drove to the only other place that came to mind—the restaurant. I screeched into the parking lot and jumped out of the car. I wanted to let him know that I wasn't running from him, especially since I was pissed the hell off that he had those punks jump me. He cut off the distance between the two of us just as fast as I did, and his hands were stuffed in his coat pockets.

"You wanna be brave, bitch?" he growled. He stopped about ten feet away from me. I threw my hands up in phony retreat.

"You know what, bro', I'm sorry."

"I ain't your *bro'*. And you cain't apologize for hittin' a nigga over the head wit a bottle, asshole. You gotta pay your dues."

"I ain't sorry for that," I said, my chest heaving furiously.

"Well, what the fuck you sorry for then?"

"I'm sorry that I'm gonna have to fuck you up like I did your friends and then brag to them about it."

"Man, you punk-ass bi—" He took a step forward just as the blaring sirens of a police car stopped him in his tracks. The burly officer with snow-white hair stepped out of the car and rearranged the glasses on his bulbous nose.

“Problem, gentlemen?” he asked looking from me to Baldy.

“No,” we barked in unison.

“It seemed like there was a problem when I saw you two fly into this parking lot like two bats outta hell.” Baldy sucked his teeth and looked at everything around him but the officer. “What’s your name, son?” he asked me.

“Chris.”

“And you?” he said, gesturing towards Baldy.

“Man, I ain’t do nothin’.”

“Never said you did, just asked for your name.”

Baldy let out a small huff. “Theodore.” I fought to hide the smirk that touched my lips when I thought of Alvin and the Chipmunks. Plus, my mouth was beginning to ache from any sort of movement. If the officer could see the lumps that were bound to pop up all over my face, he would know that the both us were lying anyhow.

“Listen, you look like you’re ready to fight and you look like you just got done. Now, I’m only gonna say this once—I don’t know what the two of you are so angry about, but I want you to go on home before it gets worse. If you leave with me, it definitely will." Baldy didn't seem as though he wanted to go to jail today and I damned sure didn't. He turned defeatedly and headed back to his car. Baldy paused and glanced over his shoulder.

"See you around, Chris."

"Can't wait."

Chapter 11

I reached across the booth and shook hands with the chef I had just hired. His name was Thomas Rizzo, and he was a graduate of Johnson and Wales with twelve years of experience. I knew I was jumping the gun a bit by hiring a chef so soon, but that was first priority to me. Besides, I didn't mind keeping my interview with him, because I got out of that ass-kicking with nothing more than minor bruises.

I attempted to call Sylvia since I hadn't spoken to her for about two days, but I didn't get an answer at the house or on her cell phone. I pulled out a yellow slip of paper with Connie's number on it and called her, hoping that Gary didn't pick up the phone.

"Hello?" she whispered.

"Connie, it's Chris. Can you speak up? I can barely hear you."

"Uncle Gary's sleeping," she said uncomfortably. Just the sound of his name infuriated me. "I have to take him somewhere later on because he doesn't drive and . . . I would hate for him to wake up in a bad mood."

"Oh. Well, I was wondering if you wanted to grab a bite to eat with me? It's my treat this time."

"I would love that. I can't get out of here until the afternoon though."

"How about two?"

"That's fine. I'll meet you at the restaurant."

$$$$

Connie asked about the small bruises as soon as she saw me, but I told her that some young punks in the neighborhood tried to take my wallet and got in one good punch before running off. Of course, I threw in that I had put up a hell of a fight. There was no sense in involving her in something that wasn't her concern.

It wasn't my concern either, because I would probably never see those guys again. Just bad timing. I enjoyed Connie's company so much, I asked her if she'd like to join me for a movie too once we finished eating. Of course, she wanted to see the one with Denzel Washington, but truth be told, I didn't care what it was—I knew I wouldn't be paying much attention to the screen.

I felt like a sixteen-year-old again sitting next to Connie in the dark. Every time she shifted her legs, her denim skirt seemed to rise up her toned thighs.

I would have licked the butter from her fingers if I could. It scared me that someone I had known for less than a week intrigued me as much as Connie did. The more time I spent with her, the less time I thought of my wife at home. I had seen Connie for the past three days now, and I was looking forward to the next. Her eyes moistened towards the end of the movie, and I placed an arm around her to draw her near me. She nestled her head into my collarbone as though it belonged there.

My mind reeled with thoughts of how I could prolong the day with her. I took a peek at my watch as we exited the theater and realized that it wasn't very late at all by the time we made it back to the restaurant. Connie must have felt the same way I did, because she began to name a few places she could take me that night.

We finally agreed that she would pick me up at nine o'clock. We planned to go out dancing at a popular spot in Waterside Mall called Jillian's—the huge sports bar flaunted an arcade for the kids and a nightclub named Mojo's for the adults. She told me that the d.j. played good hip-hop music. That didn't bother me because I listened to pretty much everything besides country music, and I was willing to go anywhere as long as it was with her. I wondered what Vince would say if he knew what I was doing. He would probably give me a thumbs-up. *But I'm not like him*, I convinced myself. Besides the short-lived incident at Addiction, Connie and I hadn't done anything wrong. Not yet.

Chapter 12

Connie and I impatiently looked for parking in the cluttered garage, and I uttered a sigh of relief when I found a spot on the fourth floor. We took the elevator down to the bridge that adjoined the parking garage and Waterside Mall. We walked over the bridge and a couple of drunken white sailors and a few young black men whooped and hollered as we passed them. I was glad that I had worn tinted shades to the club that night, because I gave all of them dirty looks. I couldn't figure out why, because she didn't belong to me. I guess I couldn't really blame them, because if I were a stranger who passed her by that particular night, I would've stared too.

Connie was on fire donning a tight, black dress that stopped just above her knees and was cinched at the waist. Her hair was swept up in the back and her sex appeal rose with each step she took. Connie was all class and not a lot of ass—I had to respect her for not carrying herself as a stripper. Once we made it into the club, Jay-Z blared from the speakers and the smoke floated around us in a thick fog. I laughed at some of the liquor-induced gyrating I witnessed. Connie's face appeared to me within the passing billows, at times taking a sip of her mimosa, and every other time appearing more sedated.

"I'm ready to dance," she said, gripping my hand and leading me out to the dance floor. Now I may be white, but contrary to popular belief, I have rhythm. Connie seemed pleased, anyway, as I followed the sway of her ass and held her hands above her head. She took the lead, weaving her voodoo around me and tickling the back of my neck with that sweet breath. Our tapestry of secrets yet to come unfolded on that dance floor . . .

Her breasts pressed delicately into my back, and she dropped her hands to my waist. Connie prodded me to move in sync with her. I brought my hand back behind the back of her head and gripped the nape just below her soft locks.

"Chris?" We both jumped at the sound of my name. I spun around and a petite, chocolate-kissed woman waved at me as she headed our way. "You don't remember me, do you?" she said as she stood in front of me. No, I didn't, and that was making me nervous, because she knew who I was. Not to mention I was more than a little pissed off at the interruption. I tilted my head to the side as I tried to recall her name. "It's Karen. Remember, we met at that Christmas party last year, the one you and Sylvia came to? Me and your wife used to work together at the district attorney's office."

I wanted to run into the closest corner and hide. Here I was bumping and grinding with another woman, and an ex-associate of my wife's probably saw the whole thing. From the way she was looking at Connie, she must not have liked what she saw either. Connie placed her hands on her hips and stood her ground. Her bottom lip poked out defensively.

"Oh yeah, Karen. How have you been?" What the hell was *she* doing here?

"I've been good. I'm at a different office now. Just vacationing this week. How's the restaurant business treating you?"

"It's great. I can't complain." I wanted her to go away, but I was trying to be civil about it.

"How is Sylvia anyway? I lost her number, and I changed mine, so we haven't been able to keep in touch," she said. Karen completely ignored Connie, and Connie grew tired of her. She took a sideways step in front of me.

"Hi, I'm Constance," she said, and gave Karen's hand a limp shake. "I'm a local chef, and Chris and I have been collaborating on opening up a restaurant in Virginia Beach. So, if you're wondering what Chris is doing here with such an alluring woman who isn't his wife, I assure you, it's strictly business—no fucking involved."

Karen stiffened, opened her mouth to say something, then turned around and stalked off. I decided that it was getting too stuffy in there for me, and I didn't want to run into any old acquaintances again. Connie and I walked out onto the adjoining balcony, and I winced at the dark shadow that played across her demure face.

"I can't believe what you just said to that woman." Connie's smug smile was enough to assure me that she didn't feel guilty about it.

"I thought it was very rude of her not to acknowledge me. Then to give me all that attitude like we were doing something."

"You can't exactly blame her, Connie. How would it have looked to you?"

"Like a man and a woman dancing."

"Yeah, and that woman wasn't my wife. You know, it's funny to me how you can go from being as sweet as pie to as cold as ice when somebody pisses you off."

"When have I ever been cold?"

"Connie, you tried to sleep with me to make Vince jealous—I'm his cousin for godsake."

"I thought we were past that."

"We are. It's just that—"

"Look, Chris, when you've led the life that I have, being cold becomes second nature." I figured this was as good a time as any to ask her some personal qucstions, since she was giving me an open invitation.

"Does that have anything to do with the accident?" Her dark eyes narrowed and turned a fierce black. They looked like two pieces of coal.

"What accident?"

"You told me that your brother died in an accident."

"No, I didn't. I told you that he died but
I didn't say how." Connie gave me a deadly stare that scared me more than the two thugs who had tried to kick my ass.

"Who have you been talking to?" she yelled. My eyes took note of everyone who had put down their drinks to enjoy the show.

"Connie, I was just worried that—"

"Did Gary tell you something? What did he say?"

"Gary didn't tell me anything."

"Then how the hell did you know how my brother was killed?"

"I . . . I paid these kids on the street to tell me more about you." She cocked her head back and curled her upper lip.

"You did what? What kind of sick sonofabitch are you?"

"Connie, you don't understand." For lack of better judgment, I placed my hands on either of her arms. She wriggled free.

"Take me home."

"Connie—"

"Now!" Connie walked away from me, and I tried to brush off the snickers that rang out around us. "White boy don't know what he got."

"He damned sure cain't handle no sis-tah."

"She too much for him."

Maybe they were right. Connie's life was far more complicated than mine, but she intrigued me. I couldn't seem to stay away from her. I didn't want to stay away from her.

$$$$

We were headed back to the car, Connie's face a beet red and her mouth one, thin line of silence. She saw it before I did. I could tell by the way her body shrunk back and her angry strut faltered. There was a furry white lump on the hood of her car. We drew closer. A river of blood flowed across the hood of the Camaro and dripped down to the asphalt.

A yelp caught in the middle of Con-nie's throat, and I gripped her arm to pull her behind me. "Let me find out what the hell that is," I said and quickly surveyed the parking lot for the person who had placed the bleeding mass on her car. I slowly approached the car because, much like Connie, I wasn't anxious about making the discovery either. I picked up a lone beer bottle that lay near one of her tires and prodded the white fur with it. The carcass made a slight turn, and I wretched.

Someone had slashed the cat's neck so badly that its head hung by a shred of tissue. The blood poured freely now. Connie screamed. The vomit wouldn't come, so I lifted my head, noticing for the first time the note wedged in between the windshield wipers. I snatched it and scanned the paper briefly. It read:

Stay away from my pussy or end up like the one on her car.

Chapter 13

Connie and I didn't even contact the police. We were in such a hurry to get out of there for fear that the perpetrator still lurked around. We had grabbed some old rags from her trunk and gotten rid of the sticky mess as best as we could. Now, Connie paced the floor of Vince's condo until I poured her a glass of wine and convinced her to sit down.

"Who would do that, Connie? Maybe an old boyfriend? Somebody from the club? You know these men have crazy fixations nowadays."

"I know who did it." She looked up at me fearfully.

"Who?"

"It was Gary."

"Gary? Your uncle? How can you be so sure?"

"Because he . . . he's done stuff like this before."

"Leaving dead animals on your car?" Connie shook her head, the soft curls around her face loose and rampant now. A bronze Medusa.

"No, nothing like that. Just other crazy stuff." I kneeled down to her eye level and took her hand.

"Connie, what's going on between you and your uncle?"

I smelled the pungent odor of sweat and Egyptian musk mingling as Connie's nerves got the best of her. Much like the day I stopped by to drop off her wallet, she wouldn't look at me. The Persian rug, a vase from Mexico—she sought out everything except the hazel eyes that caressed her own, and I wiped away the wetness pooling above her upper lip with my thumb.

"Gary is sick." Her voice was so low you could hear the proverbial pin drop. "His wife, Carol, my mom's sister, battled lupes for a long time. When she died, he didn't have any other family so he was always stopping around our house. My parents would be at work, and he would watch me and my brother sometimes. I . . . at first I liked it when he came over and would bring me and Keith candy or ice cream. But then one day—"

She stopped abruptly and I expected her to end the conversation.

But she continued as though whatever heartache she felt was soothed by the release of her inner demons.

"Keith was outside playing basketball with some boys from the neighborhood. Gary called me into the den because he wanted me to watch something on the t.v. with him. I was about nine. He sat me on his lap and hugged me and told me how pretty I was, how much I reminded him of Aunt Carol." I shivered.

"He told me how much he missed her, how I was the only one that could make him *feel* better. He started kissing all on me, and I told him, begged him to stop. But he wouldn't." This time, Connie looked dead at me and I now knew why she wouldn't before—she didn't want me to see the hatred that smoldered there. "My uncle fucked me right on my mama's couch with my brother bouncing a ball in the driveway."

"Connie, you have to get out of that house." Connie shot up and snatched her hand from me.

"You think I don't know that? You think there is not one day that goes by that

I don't have to find a reason to keep on going? Every time I breath, I can feel him touching me."

"You can stay here, Connie. For the time being anyway." Connie flashed me a sad smile.

"You don't know him. Every relationship I've ever had with a man, Gary has ruined. Showing up on some of my dates, threatening the guy. I can't bring you into this even further by staying over here. Trust me, he'll find me. In Gary's fucked up world, I'm his woman. When my family was killed, I had no choice but to stay with him, and I still don't."

"Well, what about one of the girls from the club? Couldn't they let you crash with them a few nights?" She laughed dryly.

"Those catty bitches? Please. They're jealous enough as is that I'm going back to school."

"I can't let you go back there tonight, Connie." Connie picked her bag up off the end table and gently pecked my cheek.

"Leave it alone, Chris. This was a warning. It just means I can't make the same mistake again."

"What mistake?" Connie headed towards the door before the words even escaped from her mouth.

"We can't see each other anymore, Chris."

Chapter 14

If curiosity killed the cat, then I was as good as dead. I couldn't stand the way things had gone down with Connie, and I couldn't for the life of me stop wondering what Gary was doing to her. I barely heard anything the babbling idiot from the Department of Health was talking about. I had gone there to review some things, because I wanted to become more familiar with the restaurant regulations in the state of Virginia. Of course, all I wanted to do was drive to Addiction as soon as I left.

$$$$

I didn't want her to see me, to think I was checking up on her. I knew that Connie had her weaknesses, but I doubted she would let anyone pity her. I took a seat at a table in the darkest corner I could find. The fog that wafted around me carried the fragrance of different women, each with their own language. I couldn't understand what any of them were saying to me. Connie's sweat and perfume were now my native tongue. I knew who Connie was the minute I saw her entertaining a gentleman on the other side of the room. She wore a black wig this time. The look was different, but the languid movements were the same. I studied the sweet percussion of her hips and realized that my heart was beating to the same rhythm.

"Why you over here in the dark by yourself, baby?" came the voice dripping of thick molasses to my right. I snatched my eyes away from Connie in mild annoyance to see who my unwanted visitor might be. A petite, light-complexioned stripper with green, almond-shaped eyes tried to draw me in with the thrust of her pelvis. There was no way in hell I wanted to see another man indulge in what I so badly wanted from Connie, so I gave the broad the benefit of the doubt. I didn't need to tell her what to do as I slid a bill in between her hip and g-string.

"I'm Billie Jean." She seemed to like the direct approach.

"That's an interesting name." She giggled.

"My mom was a big Michael Jackson fan." As though that were enough talking for her, Billie Jean swung her ass into my face and threw it back with the wildness of a possessed woman. She wasn't half-bad. In fact, she was a nice diversion for the moment.

"Let's take this party elsewhere," she mouthed over the loud music.

I allowed her to lead me into that separate room, dejavous wreaking havoc in my mind as I thought of the first time Connie did that. The same bouncer stood there, but I could tell he didn't recognize me, because I received the once-over again. Billie Jean bathed my face with the mass of hair that swung down her back. I wondered if she came from any Asian descent. I really didn't have time to ask her, because as she turned around to place her legs on either side of my hips, her face took on a distorted look of pain. Billie Jean fell back, and her head smacked the floor with a thud. I jumped up, shocked to see that Connie still had a good hold on the end of the other girl's hair.

"You fucking bitch!" Connie cried. Billie Jean squirmed on the floor as Connie sat atop her, clawing at her face. Billie Jean held her arms up helplessly to protect her head. I briefly stared at the two in awe then scooped Connie up by her waist.

“Get the fuck off me, Chris!” she cried. She had become a fierce panther, almost overpowering me with defiance. Billie Jean took advantage of the situation and smashed her palm into the side of Connie’s face.

“You nasty, little whore! Don’t you ever put your hands on me again!” Billy Jean hollered.

She raised her hand to strike Connie once more, but Rodney caught her wrist in midair and dragged her out of the room on her heels. Billie Jean unraveled a string of profanities as Rodney sneered at the two of us.

“Control your bitch, man,” he yelled. “I’m goin’ to get the owner.”

Connie staggered into my arms and laid her head on my shoulder. I couldn’t see the whites of her eyes because they were too bloodshot. Something was seriously wrong with her. And I knew that it wasn’t just a battle with jealousy either. I shook Connie hard and forced her to look at me. She blinked twice.

“How much did you drink?” I asked. The owner entered the room with Rodney at his side. The lines etched into his face may as well have been arrows directing us to get the hell out of his club. He was surprisingly cool about it.

"I'm Curtis Monroe, the owner of Addiction. I want you to take your little girlfriend to get her shit out of my dressing room, and I don't ever want her to set foot in this club again. I warned her the last time."

"The last time?" His laugh was brittle.

"You don't know? This ain't the first time Candy has finished a few bottles on *my* time. When you go get her shit, you'll see what I'm talking about. Now, you can come here anytime you please, but this bitch is not welcomed back."

I lifted Connie up into my arms.

"I'll take a raincheck. Where's the dressing room?" Rodney led me there, and a very weak Connie pointed to her locker. I put her down so that I could open it while she leaned against the others.

A couple of her costumes toppled out onto the floor. Amidst the mess were four small flasks of Hennessy. I picked up one that was half-empty.

"You're drunk as hell, aren't you?" Connie's ashen face suddenly burned with shame.

"Why are you even here, Chris? I thought I told you I didn't want to see you anymore!"

"Well, that's besides the point right now, isn't it, Connie?" I stuffed the flask into my blazer pocket and pushed the clothes into
her black duffle bag. "You are going home."

"No, he's still there . . ."

I shot her a nasty look and sunk my fingers into her forearm.

"Look at you! Do you feel sexy? What the hell would make you think to get drunk so that a whole bunch of men can take advantage of you more than thcy usually would?" She began to sob and buried her face inside of her hands. I didn't mean to scream at her, but she needed to hear what I had to say.

"It was Gary!" she cried.

"What did he do to you?"

"The same thing he always does, Chris. I only drink like this when he gets ready to go on his gambling trips. I swear."

"For what, Connie?"

"He always starts touching me whenever he gets ready to go away for the weekend. Starts with that bullshit about how he's gonna be *missing* me. I can't take it when he does that, Chris! That," she said, pointing at the flask I had placed in my pocket, "makes it all go away." I folded my arms around her and felt the fresh tears seep through my shirt.

"That does not make it go away, Connie. It's just like being in a dream. And then you wake up." Connie cast her red eyes up at me. I remembered my mother looking at me the same way about twenty-five years before. I couldn't save her from an early demise, because I was too young, but maybe I could save Connie. I wouldn't let a man become the death of her too.

Chapter 15

Since I knew Gary was still home, I asked Connie to stay at Vince's condo for the night. I told her we would pick up her car from the club in the morning. Gary wouldn't find her at the condo, and even if he did, he would be on my territory, and I was going to knock his fucking head off. In the meantime, I wanted to help her make some other living arrangements. She had to get over her fear of leaving Gary.

I drew Connie a hot, sudsy bath and lathered her up. The droplets of water running down her back shone like a river against Egyptian clay. I dried Connie off and put her into my guest bed. She conked right out and I stood at the door for a moment watching her sleep. I went into the bathroom and flushed the remainder of her cognac down the toilet. My cell buzzed at my hip.

"Hello?"

"Chris?" I had forgotten how sexy Sylvia's voice could sound after waking up from a nap. That was her usual routine after going to the gym in the evening.

"Yeah, it's me, baby. What's going on?"

"Chris . . . I miss you." Now that was a shock to me. It had been a while since Sylvia expressed herself to me emotionally or otherwise, unless it was out of anger.

"I miss you, too."

"I know we've been arguing a lot lately but—"

"Chris?" My heart leapt at the sound of Connie's tired voice behind me. She stood there in the nude, rubbing her eyes. "Oh, I'm sorry. I didn't know you were on the phone."

Connie went back into the guest room, and I returned to my conversation, praying that Sylvia hadn't heard her.

"Chris?" By the way Sylvia's tone changed, I knew she had. "Who was that?"

Damn.

"That was Connie," I said evenly.

"Who is Connie?" I chuckled to lighten the mood.

"You know, one of Vince's girls. He wanted her to ask me something."

"Oh."

I could hear her relaxing over the phone. “Well, I hope you come home soon.”

“I can’t wait to see you when I do.”

“I love you, Chris.”

“I love you, too, Sylvia.” We hung up, and I thought of how that reminded me of old times when we were first married. It also made me wonder, with some guilt, what I was doing with a naked woman sleeping in my bed that wasn’t Sylvia. For the first time since I came down here, I realized how wrong all of this was. I wanted to help Connie, but I knew that I could no longer put my marriage at risk. I went into the guest-room to see what she wanted.

She was wide awake with her knees up to her chin. I sat on the side of the bed. Connie looked like such a child to me as the moonlight touched her through the blinds. I didn’t know how I was going to help her and then break off what this relationship between us had become.

“Are you okay?” I asked.

“Yeah. I just need some stuff from my house. I know it’s asking a lot but—”

"No, Connie. I don't feel comfortable going over there. And you are in no condition to be going anywhere anyhow."

"I could give you the key."

"Hell no."

"Gary should be gone by now, if that's what you're worried about."

"I don't give a shit! I don't feel right going into that sick bastard's house."

"I just want to get some stuff while he's gone. Plus, I got school on Monday, and I'm gonna have to start looking for a new job. I'll never get away from him without either of the two." I gave in when she put it that way. Connie handed me the key, and I told her that I remembered how to get there.

Chapter 16

On my way to Norfolk, I considered turning around several times. Before I knew it, I was parked in front of Connie's house and it was dark as hell outside. I climbed the steps to the porch and searched for the keyhole. I went inside, and this time, the stale stench of mothballs and beer greeted me. No doubt these two odors had rolled off of Gary's fat ass.

I found the stairway light switch and climbed my way to the second floor. Connie said that her room would be the third one on the right. I realized this was the first time I had ever been in her room, and she wasn't even here with me.

I flipped on a small lamp by her bed side and snooped around. Her room was where all the other pictures were. I saw a photo of a little boy who shared Connie's caramel skin and deep smile—he was probably her brother. Then there was a picture of Connie and two people who looked to be her parents walking along the boardwalk at the beach—she couldn't have been any more than five, and there was ice cream smeared all over her face. I laughed out loud at that one. I saw a picture in a frame of Connie and another woman hugging each other, but the other half of the picture was ripped off.

I turned the frame over. *Connie, Auntie Carol, and Uncle Gary, Christmas 1989*. Well, I figured out who was on the other half of the photo.

Connie really was the spitting image of Carol but far more beautiful. I pulled the suitcase Connie told me about out from underneath her bed and started loading it with her belongings. Lastly, I grabbed the picture of the little boy and the picture of Connie with her parents and placed them in the suitcase too. I hoisted the bag full of her college books over one shoulder and slid the suitcase down the stairs. I hoped I wasn't forgetting anything, because I didn't plan on coming back.

$$$$

I figured I would have time to stop for a cigarette—a habit that I rarely indulged in unless I was out of fine cigars—at a gas station I had passed around the corner. The

East Indian man behind the counter nodded his "hello" to me as I headed to the back where I could grab a bottle of juice—my mouth had gone dry after heaving Connie's things down the stairs and out to the trunk of my car. The bottle slipped from my hand and rolled down the aisle that housed the cookies and chips.

"Shit," I muttered and bent down to pick it up. I could hear the chime over the door as customers scurried in and out, buying items and paying for gas. Then, a sudden quiet blanketed the place.

I stood up and ducked immediately. But I couldn't ignore what I had seen. I could hide all I wanted to, and the cashier would still be standing there in wide-eyed terror as the gun taunted his face. I heard the two gunmen barking out there orders for money as I sweated my ass off at the back of the aisle.

I looked to my left and saw an elderly, black woman quivering in the corner on the other side of the store. I lifted a finger to my lips and she nodded. She shut her eyes tightly, and I did the same. A shot rang out and we both jumped, neither one of us making a sound. There went the chime over the door.

I rose and peered over the top of the aisle. The cashier was slumped over the counter, clawing for the phone. The gun he had pulled—and didn't get a chance to use—was still in his other hand. The gunmen were gone. I dashed to the front of the store, hoping that they weren't going to pay us another unexpected visit.

I dialed 911, and the cashier whispered the address. I couldn't understand the breathless words. The wound to his arm didn't look too bad, but the blood was making a waterfall over the side of the counter. I told the operator to hold on, and I rushed outside of the store to find the address. I saw the 9mm Glock before I felt it. The cold, hard metal drilled a hole into the side of my temple. I imagined what a bullet would do.

"Talk some shit now, mothafucka," came the familiar voice.

Chapter 17

"**Where are you** taking me?" I asked the two masked men in the front of the car. Neither said a word. I got a good look at the black Honda Civic—I didn't know which year—before they threw me in and knocked my cell phone to the ground. Too bad I didn't see the license plate, but for all I knew, the car could have been stolen.

I knew that Baldy was the one who pulled the gun on me although I couldn't see his face. I couldn't seem to stop running into the guy, so I came to the conclusion that he must live somewhere in or nearby Connie's neighborhood. He was driving too quickly for me to figure out where we were going—the buildings and street-lights flew by in a blur. Five minutes later, we began to slow down.

The perspiration boiled along my fore-head when I realized we were headed to-wards the restaurant. What the hell were they planning to do? For the first time since any of my unfortunate run-ins with Baldy, I was more than a little worried, though I didn't show it. In fact, I was sick to my stomach with fear, knowing that the next place I might lay my head would be inside of a body bag. It had turned into more than just a scuffle between two men. The stagnant malice hanging in the air let me know that Baldy would have his vengeance very soon. Apparently, I had hit the wrong man over the head. I tried reasoning with them again.

"What is it that you want? More money?" I heard the harsh, muffled laugh in front of me.

"No." At least he had said something. The quiet was driving me crazier than anything else.

"Well, what then?"

"I want to keep a promise." We pulled into the parking lot where the restaurant stood. Baldy came to a screeching halt and pulled me from the backseat with the gun digging into my lower back. He drew back his huge palm and shoved me onto the asphalt.

The gravel ripped my shirt to shreds, and instinctively, I turned onto my back with my scraped hands held high.

"Don't do this." Baldy laughed again.

"What, asshole? You think we gonna kill you? Hell to the no. I got somethin' far better planned. Gimme the key to this spot." I feigned ignorance and shook my head.

"I don't have it on me."

"Pat him down," he instructed his partner. The other man dug through my pockets and pulled out a chain of keys. I knew that one of them had the name of the restaurant on it, and now, they did too. Baldy pointed his gun at me and cocked it.

"I hate liars." He brought a finger to his chin with his free hand. "But you know what? Liar, liar, pants on fire." He turned to his partner. "Take him inside, and I'll be back in a few." His partner gave me the key, grabbed me by the hair, and forced me towards the entrance. Baldy jumped back in the car and took off down the street.

"Open it," his partner said to me once we had reached the front of the building. I unlocked the door, and we went inside. Only the light from the full moon lit up the place. We stood by the entrance, and he held the gun on me until Baldy returned about twenty minutes later. Baldy walked right by us without so much as a "kiss my ass" and held a kerosene can in the air for me to see. He sloshed the liquid against any wall he could find and lit a match. Baldy threw it into the closest pool of kerosene, and my heart sank as I watched the place start to burn. His friend dragged me out of there, and Baldy quickly followed suit. He clapped his hands like a giddy toddler.

"Somebody had to teach your ass a lesson." He chuckled. The fire that gleamed in my eyes wasn't a reflection of the restaurant. My fear had died down, and my temper flared.

"I'm gonna kill you!" I said, leaping on top of him. Baldy fell back in surprise, and the gun slid out of his hand and skidded across the parking lot. His partner struggled to pull me off of Baldy, because my hands were planted firmly around his neck. His partner resorted to pulling the gun on me again, and my brief moment of insanity withered away.

I was mad as hell, but I didn't want to die that night. Afterwards, I thought Baldy was going to kill me for sure, but he brushed himself off in disgust. At least he had stopped laughing.

“I should blow your damned brains out right now, but I got what I wanted. Let’s get the hell outta here, man, ‘fore somebody call the cops,” he told his partner. They both jumped into the Honda Civic, and I read the plates before they sped off—BAD MF.

Chapter 18

The officer patted me on the back. "You alright, man?" he asked. My place was burning to a crisp, and I was far from alright. The fire engines were deafening and only contributed to my migraine. Paramedics flitted around me like mosquitoes and incited my anger by asking me if I was okay every five minutes. A ripped shirt and a few scrapes on my hands were the least of my concerns.

The police had fired questions at me about the shooting and robbing at the gas station, plus my brief kidnapping. They wanted to know why the suspects burned my place down. I told them about the bar fight at Addiction, but unfortunately, the police decided that it could have been any one of Baldy's friends who committed the arson. I wouldn't be able to blame it solely on Baldy.

I stubbed out my cigarette along the curb I sat on—a sympathetic passerby had given it to me. It appeared that Baldy had gotten his payback and was probably going to get away with it. Although Baldy did look like a "BAD MF" right now as the Honda's license plates had suggested, the car was stolen. I couldn't prove anything. Even if any of the patrons in the gas station recognized Baldy's voice, they might be too afraid to talk.

"Well, I'm keeping it together. I'm mad as hell right now, but at least I'm alive, and nobody else was hurt."

"They say that cashier's gonna be okay. You did the right thing." I was glad that someone felt that way. I thought to call my cousin but I didn't want to worry him while he was away. I also had to figure out what I was going to do about Connie, so I couldn't have him rushing down here.

One thing was for sure—my plans for opening up a second restaurant were out of the question. If there were signs telling me to hold off on the restaurant, the arson was certainly the biggest one. That night, two enemies endangered my life, and they still walked the streets having done far worse things than Larry Pantone.

There was no way I was looking for another building in Virginia Beach knowing that. I guess Sylvia's intuition was right, and nothing hurt as much as my pride. It sucked and I was fucked. Forced to watch my new place go up in flames while I couldn't do a damned thing. Worst of all, I had to go home and tell my wife. It would be a good reason for her to object to me coming back to Virginia altogether—I knew she wanted me to see less of my pussy-hungry cousin to begin with.

Although Sylvia would act disappointed for me, it would be her own secret triumph. No trips out of town. A busy husband, but at least a busy husband close by in New York. I hated the taste of defeat, but it was a gagging pill I had to swallow.

$$$$

The officer gave me a ride back to the gas station—he talked to me about how lucky I was to be alive. As I listened to him, my perspective changed about the events of that night. Perhaps everything that happened was meant to drive me back home to my wife. Maybe I had denied her too long.

Police tape blocked the gas station like an intricate vein around a still heart. An officer handed over my phone, which was surprisingly in tact, and I headed straight for my car. I knew I looked like I had fallen off of a building, but I didn't care. I decided to get Connie the hell out of Vince's place, and as soon as my car was ready, I was driving home. I wouldn't abandon her. I would even put her in a hotel if I had to, but my ass was gone. My newfound motto? Make money at Balducci's, make love at home.

$$$$

When I arrived back at the condo, it was nearly two a.m. I had left about four hours ago and expected Connie to be tucked away in the bed. Instead, she sat on the couch with her legs crossed underneath one of my oversized t-shirts. Her red eyes scanned me from head to toe, and I watched her jaw drop. She ran from the couch and held me in a tight embrace.

"I was so worried about you," she said. "I called your phone and some guy said that there had been a robbery and . . ." Her voice caught.

"It's okay," I whispered into her hair.

"Are you hurt?" She took a step back and studied me.

"It's just a few scratches." Connie led me to the couch and I told her everything that had happened. She shook her head.

"That asshole, Theo, is the local thug. His pastime is robbing people. If I had known what went down at the club, I never would've sent you over there." Connie stroked my cheek. "Seems like he always beats the system. Beats his girlfriend, too. Always coming to the club with black eyes talking about how she fell down the steps or some shit. I've never seen him do something this big though."

"What about the girlfriend? You think she'll talk? I mean she's gotta know where he's hiding."

"Yeah, right. Tanya is too afraid." I rubbed my tired eyes and looked at Connie. I knew she had been crying and worrying about what may have happened to me, so telling her that she had to leave would be slightly harder now. But I had convinced myself on the way to the condo that Connie was not my problem and that she could make it on her own. I barely knew her well enough to remain concerned. God knows I had been in enough trouble behind her.

"Connie, we have to talk."

"I know what it's about, Chris."

"You do?"

"Tonight, I was scared to death that something had happened to you. It made me realize, too . . . how much I care about you." Before I could respond, she leaned in and planted her lips firmly on mine. My mind told me to pull away, to go on with what I had to say to her. But as she massaged my tongue with her own, the words became a distant memory. The temptation I had fought for so long finally caught me with a right hook. I yanked my tee over Connie's head with a longing I had never known and watched as she removed what was left of my tattered shirt.

My lips sought out her nipples, blackberries bursting inside my mouth. My hand dipped low for the milk and honey I always knew flowed between her legs and now drenched my fingers. I wanted to drink from there, to lap up every drop and let the taste linger on my tongue.

Connie gasped as I followed the mingling scent of her pheromones, sweat, and a new perfume I couldn't name. I tugged at the delicate skin along her inner thighs with my teeth, watching as her hands clawed for an invisible piece of something to grip. She finally settled on my hair as I sunk my face into her buried treasure.

"Chris," she moaned, resting her calves on the nape of my neck. Connie squirmed in an effort to get away, but I tightened the firm grip I had on her ass. I plunged my tongue between her pussy lips as though nothing else would have filled my appetite. I enjoyed the soft sounds she made in A minor, then A sharp, then an extended B flat. "Yes, Chris! Yeah, baby! Ooohh, that shit feels so good."

She called on every powerful being in the sky as her body shook and her storm released its rain all over me. I gently grabbed her ankles to remove her legs from my neck then kissed her mouth again so that she could enjoy what I had. I didn't want to take Connie on the couch, so I lifted her, and she instinctively cuffed her legs around my waist. Our lips moved in sync for so long that neither of us could breathe by the time I carried her over to Vince's countertop. The thought of protection crossed my mind as Connie undid my belt buckle. She looked at me and must have known what I was thinking. Stop. We knew that we couldn't continue groping each other because being responsible would be thrown out the window.

"Vince keeps some in the top drawer of that end table."

I found the pack of gold Magnums, took one from the box, and regained my position in between her dangling legs. Connie slid my pants and briefs downward and watched me roll the condom on. Her bottom lip quivered as though something wasn't right. I knew it wasn't the size of my dick, because I had never had any complaints.

"What is it?"

"I want this, Chris, it's just . . ."

"Did I do something wrong?"

"I just don't want you to think that I'm nasty. It's different right now, with you."

"Why would I think that?"

"You know, with Vince and me having been together. Then Gary touching me the way that he does. I just . . . I feel dirty sometimes."

"Look, Connie. I may have judged you before, but I don't now. I know that you have made the wrong choices for the right reasons, and I also know that there is more to you than just this," I said, and ran my hand from her collarbone to the spot on her thigh just above her knee. "I'm not Vince, and I damned sure ain't Gary, and I want to show you what it means to touch a woman." I suckled on her earlobe. "To make love to one."

The visible tension in Connie's body melted away, and I didn't take my time plunging inside of her. Connie nearly bucked off of the countertop as she met my thrusts head on. I kept my eyes locked on hers the whole time.

"Give it to me baby—harder!"

"Dammit, Connie! Oh God, your pussy feels so good!"

"Come on, Chris. Come with me, baby." Her voice had taken on a seductive lilt, and she wound her hips with determination.

"Yes, Connie . . . oh, shit!" I felt like someone exploded inside of me. Her body sipped on my slow release as I collapsed on top of her. I couldn't tell where she started and I began.

Chapter 19

When Connie and I woke up, we were entangled on the carpet in front of the fireplace. Quick flashes of Connie on her hands and knees, Connie mounting and riding me like a horse, and Connie's back being ground into the floor went through my head. I felt my dick harden, thinking about how Connie had ended my peaked curiosity when she went down on me with that full mouth. We had gone at it for hours, and I was starting to feel it. I was so groggy that I didn't even hear the doorknob turn. Vince nearly stumbled over his own dropped jaw.

"Well, what the hell do we have here?"

Connie awoke at the sound of his voice, and the blood rushed to her face and mine. She quickly looked around for anything that she could cover herself up with although Vince had probably seen her naked several times.

When he gave her a smug smile, Connie resorted to dashing upstairs. I stood up and tugged on my pants that lay on the other side of the room. Anything not to have to face Vince and the smart remarks I knew he was going to hurl at me.

I had never betrayed my marriage before, and I had always given Vince flak about settling down. He had said that my time would come eventually. I didn't know that he would catch me red-handed and red everywhere else.

"You know, this is kind of funny, Chris." He dropped his bags on the floor and followed me around the couch.

"What's funny about it?"

"You talk all this shit about how much you love Sylvia, and I find you here with this hooker."

"First off, my wife is my business, and secondly, Connie is not a hooker," I snapped.

"Whoa. Are you getting testy over this broad?" I didn't answer him and he knew I wasn't in the mood for his wise ass mouth. "Look Chris, I'm not gonna judge you. You just watch that one, okay? She's been through some shit. It's messed with her head."

"How would you know? Did you two talk as you kicked her out of bed?"

"I know you're not getting pussy-whipped. Connie and me, it was just sex. You're acting like you caught feelings."

"I can handle my dick, thank you. I've been doing it ever since I learned how to piss. And I'm well aware of Connie's shit. What Connie and I did is what we did anyway. I'm going home."

"What about the restaurant?"

"There is no restaurant."

"What do you mean 'there is no restaurant'?"

"Exactly what I said. The shit should be burnt to a crisp by now."

"What?"

"You heard me. I had the pleasure of standing there to watch."

I relayed the news to him, starting with the very night I hit Baldy over the back of the head. I had never seen Vince that serious, not to mention angry. It seemed like he was even more pissed than I was.

"Something told me to come home early! We gotta find those motherfuckers, Chris! You can't let them get away with this."

"And what am I supposed to do when I find them, hell, if I find them? The police can't even question them, because they don't even know where the hell they are."

"I have money, Chris. You have money. It won't be hard."

"Hell no, Vince. I got a wife and another business to think about."

"They threaten your life and burn down your spot and you're just gonna brush this shit under the rug? What the hell happened to the kid I knew from Camden?"

"He grew the fuck up, Vincent! This is not a game. We're not kids anymore. I have a lot more to lose now so just leave it alone."

"Fine. I'll leave it alone. But if you change your mind, just let me know. This time, I'll be completely sober." We were quiet for a moment, but I had already made up my mind.

A long time ago, I may have been an angry fool looking to spill some blood, but I had grown into a man. The insurance claim wouldn't help me forget about the arson but neither would going to jail. The only other thing I would try to forget was the huge mistake Connie and I had made the night before.

Chapter 20

Vince went straight to bed once he went upstairs, so it made things less uncomfortable for Connie before we left. I had loaded all of her things into the rental and called a Motel 6—I charged her a room for the next month. Connie wasn't ungrateful, but she was sad to see me leave. There was a space wedged between us while I took her back to the club to pick up her car.

I knew that now wasn't the time to mention the passion I had felt last night, to tell her that I was grateful that she had made me feel that way again. At the end of the day, I'd be gone. My car was ready to be picked up and I decided that I wouldn't tell Sylvia about the arson—I would tell her that she was the reason I was coming home, that I had come to my senses which was halfway true. Some of the girls that stood outside of Addiction pointed and whispered at Connie when we pulled up, and she climbed into her car. We ignored them. I transferred her things into the trunk of the Camaro, and she followed me to drop off the rental. As we headed back to Vince's, I turned to Connie. I could still smell and taste her milk and honey.

"I want you to know that last night was very special to me, Connie."

"You don't have to say that, Chris."

"I want to say it, Connie. I haven't had someone show me that much passion in a long time. Thank you for that." She tried to smile. Did she know what was coming? "Really, Connie. I do care about you. You have definitely proven to me that you can't judge a book, and that you're not one of Vince's regular girls."

"I'm through with Vince—I hope you know that. I'm tired of being disrespected by these assholes in my life, but then, I guess I let them do it."

"I love my cousin, but he's not the one for you. Excuse my language, but I'm sure you know that you have always been a piece of ass to him. No matter how good it was, he had no intention of it getting serious."

"I was just doing what I had to do to get away from Gary. Financially and otherwise. I would have rather had someone pay for it than take it from me."

Her eyes spilled over, and I was glad that we stopped so I could hold her.

"You are a smart, strong, beautiful woman, Constance. Don't ever let anyone take that away from you. Don't let alcohol do it either. Remember I said that, okay?" Connie cupped the side of my face.

"I won't forget anything about you, Chris." She covered my mouth with her own. The kiss was warm and brief, just like our affair.

Chapter 21

Since it was so early in the day, I decided I had plenty of time to choose a gift for Sylvia. Vince would follow me later so that I could pick up my car. My wife had no idea I was coming back this weekend, and I thought it would be a great surprise. I struck up the nerve to take one of Vince's cars to MacArthur Center in downtown Norfolk. I could only pray that what happened to mine didn't happen to his.

$$$$

The ritzy mall was four stories high, and I didn't know where to begin. I knew that Sylvia was a big fan of jewelry so I decided to start at Zales. My eyes rifled through the tennis bracelets on display at another jewelry store nearby. I was about to ask the sales associate for a closer look at one that had impressed me when I heard a familiar laugh over the noise of the crowd. My brow wrinkled as I searched for the person who had belted it out.

"Is there a problem sir?" the sales associate asked. I ignored him and heard the laugh again.

I turned to my right and quickened my pace as the sound grew distant. Now, I could make out the back of a woman's hourglass figure with a smaller figure at her side. The woman turned her head to her left to say something to the little boy.

Apparently it was funny, because he threw his tiny head back in amusement—I had seen Connie do the same thing in the picture of her standing by the tree. I knew it was her when she picked him up in her arms to avoid the jostle of the crowd, the hair falling away from her face. He was the little boy from the photo in her room.

I walked several feet behind, trying to keep up with a woman in stiletto heels that was moving faster than me. She stopped by a trendy store called The Z Spot and walked towards the back. I hid behind a rack of name- brand shirts and pretended as though I was looking for something. I watched as Connie approached a tall brown man with curly hair. He shared the same features as the little boy she held and bellowed like a basketball player. That made it easier for me to hear the conversation. I moved a little closer anyhow. The guy tapped his watch.

"Where the hell you been, Connie?" She rolled her eyes in disgust.

"Don't start with me, Ahmad. We're only five minutes late."

"It's been more than five minutes. I thought I told you to meet me here by eleven a.m. so that I could drop him off at the daycare and go to work. How the hell you expect me to take care of him with no damned job?"

"I'm not doing this in front of our son. 'Our' being the operative word."

"Yeah, whatever. Come on, Darren. Daddy's gotta go." Connie ignored Ahmad and hugged the little boy tightly. She showered his forehead with kisses and tickled his underarms. The little boy giggled and squirmed in her arms.

"Mommy's going to see you later, sweetie. I love you much."

"I love you too, Mommy. I'm gonna draw you a pretty picture today, okay?"

"I can't wait. I'm going to put it in a frame when I get it." A reluctant Connie handed Darren over to Ahmad and watched Ahmad stalk out of the store without so much as a goodbye. Darren waved at Connie over his father's broad shoulder, and she fought back the tears. She made her way towards the exit after they were gone, unaware that anyone had witnessed her disappointment. What really bothered me was the way she had looked at Ahmad with such longing when they argued. It almost made me forget why I had come to the mall to begin with.

I stepped out from my hiding place, and Connie stopped short of running into me. The blood drained from her face, and she placed her hands on my chest in shock.

"Chris?"

"Connie."

"I . . . did you . . ."

"Are you trying to ask me if I saw what just happened?"

"I can explain."

"You didn't tell me you had a kid. The whole time you were out here drinking and taking off your clothes for God knows who, not to mention screwing my cousin, I thought it was just your life you were ruining. I had no idea that you were ruining your child's life too. Tell me, Connie, are you fucking Ahmad as well?"

The slap she gave me could be heard all over the store, and the side of my face stung like hell. The Chinese owners glared at us as though we had better not cause a scene in their store. They didn't have to worry, because Connie stomped away from me, and I followed her all the way down to Nordstroms. I caught her wrist and pulled her into one of the dressing rooms with me. My tall frame blocked the door.

"You had no right to say those things to me!" she shouted.

"You're right, I didn't. But why the hell didn't you tell me you had a kid? You told me everything else."

"It was already getting complicated between us. We got too comfortable too fast and it was nice so I knew it wouldn't last long. I wasn't bringing my son into the mix." Connie lowered her voice. "You're a great man, Chris, but you're a man nonetheless."

"What the hell is that supposed to mean?"

"It means that you aren't angry about my kid."

"I don't know what you're talking about."

"Yes, you do. The way Ahmad and I were talking to each other. Obviously, there are a lot of old, unsettled feelings adding fuel to that fire."

"Yeah, that much was obvious. I thought—I didn't know you had anyone special in your life right now."

"Well, he and I have a child and a history together, Chris." Connie cocked her head to the side and furrowed her brow. "And you don't like that, do you?"

"No, I don't." I pushed the weight of my body into her and kissed her even harder than I had the night before. She kissed me back, and my hands hiked her skirt up just above her hips. I was pleased to find that she wore no panties, and I moistened my fingers with my tongue to slip them inside of her. She was already wet when she parted her legs and enveloped my hand with her promise. I spun her around and watched as she bent over and placed her hands on the seat inside the tight dressing room. She looked back at me.

"Fuck me, Chris," she said.

My chest heaved with excitement, with the anticipation of doing something I hadn't even done with my own wife. Pants dropped, briefs dropped, and I entered Connie from behind. We both ground our teeth as I pummeled her. I covered her mouth with my hand to mask her grunts and moans from the passing patrons.

Each thrust grew deeper, each quake in Connie's thighs a little stronger. I felt the rise of submission, and I pulled out of her. My smooth nature coated her backside, and Connie handed me a tissue from her purse without saying anything. I wiped myself off, wiped off her ass, and fixed my clothes. I couldn't swallow the lump in my throat that stopped me from speaking. I backed out of the dressing room and closed the door on Connie's heavy breathing. I had almost forgotten about the bracelet.

Chapter 22

I had just broken the bad news to Mr. Rizzo that I couldn't hire him as a chef at the new restaurant when Connie beeped in on my cell phone. I had finally convinced Vince that what she and I had was just one night of sex, so I took our conversation out onto the balcony. Anyhow, I didn't think he would hear me talking over the vibrator he was using on the young lady upstairs.

"Ahmad and I haven't been together in four years, Chris."

"And? I'm married. You can do as you please." I didn't really want her to do as she pleased, but there was no logical way for me to stop her. I belonged to someone else.

"Well, I just thought you might like to know. Gary was the reason why we broke up."

"Oh?"

"I told you that he is very possessive over me. He hated when Ahmad and I started seeing each other. But I was happy then. Gary stopped trying to touch me since I had Ahmad in my life—he would've beat Gary's ass if he found out what Gary was doing to me. When I got pregnant, Gary was madder than I had ever seen him. He knew for sure then that Ahmad and I were sleeping together."

"What did he do?"

"He wanted me to get rid of it, but I flat out refused. Those were the worst nine months of my life. He worked me like a slave to get back at me and said that I couldn't leave, because I had nowhere else to go. But I still had my baby."

"Why didn't you stay with Ahmad?"

"Yeah, right. Ahmad and I were still young, and he lived with his parents then. They refused to have some pregnant girl staying in their house—said it wasn't right by God. They finally came around and accepted Darren when he was born. I gave Ahmad full custody. I made up some bull-shit about me not being mentally stable enough to take on a kid, so he didn't question why I gave him custody so easily.

Besides, his parent's lived in some high- siddity neighborhood, and they had spoiled him so I knew they would spoil their grandchild. He never did find out what

Gary was doing to me, because I was too ashamed to tell him, and there was no way in hell I was raising Darren in my house."

"You two could have made it work."

"I had to start paying child support for Darren, and stripping was fast money. Ahmad broke it off with me when he found out what I was doing."

"I'm sorry I walked out on you like that, Connie. I just felt like such an asshole, because I was there to buy Sylvia a gift."

"Well, you'll be leaving tonight, so there's no possible way we can get our hands on each other again."

We both laughed without humor at that unpleasant thought, although I would fight the temptation of stopping by her room before I left. "Thanks for everything, Chris."

"Well, now that you have somewhere to stay for a few weeks, I figure you'll have time to get yourself together. Call me if you need me, okay?"

"I'll be picking my little man up from the daycare this evening and dropping him off to his daddy in the morning, so he'll be keeping me company tonight." I smiled as I thought about the little boy with Connie's grin.

$$$$

My phone vibrated, disrupting the quick nap I tried to fit in before Vince took me to pick up my car at his friend's shop that night. I glanced at the clock. I could still get two more hours of sleep if I ignored the annoying buzz. I flipped back over onto my side as though the phone would stop going off if I couldn't see it. Surprisingly, it did—at least for a few seconds. The cell began doing its little dance off the nightstand and bounced across the floor. I snatched it up.

"Yeah?" I barked into the phone.

"Oh, God! Chris, help me!" Connie screamed into my ear. She was crying hysterically, and the thudding noises in the background were deafening.

"Connie, what is it? What's wrong?" My heart pounded in my throat when I heard Darren whimpering at her side.

"Mommy, I'm scared," he said. He was sobbing now.

"He's trying to kill me!"

"Who, Connie? What the hell is going on?"

"Gary found us! I don't know how, but he found us!"

"Connie, I need you to calm down. What is all that noise?"

"He took the bus here. Gary knocked on the door while I was in the bathroom, and Darren opened it. Gary busted in like he was crazy, and Darren came running for me."

"What happened then?"

"I managed to snatch Darren up and lock us inside the bathroom. Oh my God, he's trying to tear the door down!" The banging noise was drowning Connie out now. I could hear Gary yelling at her from the bedroom.

"You can't stay in there all night, bitch! I'm gonna get in one way or the other!" he yelled.

"Connie, did you call 911?" I asked.

"He already asked me that . . . he said if he goes to jail behind my ass, he's gonna make me and my bastard son sorry!"

"Who the fuck you talkin' to, huh? Betta not be no damn police!" Gary ranted in the background.

"Please hurry, Chris. I don't know what he's gonna do if he breaks that door down."

"Don't worry, Connie. I'm on my way."

I slid my feet into my sneakers and ran down the hall to Vince's room. He was asleep on his back with some naked blonde slumped over his chest. "Vince, I need to hold your car for a second." Vince mumbled something that sounded like an okay, and I grabbed his keys off the dresser before closing the door.

Chapter 23

I had no idea what was about to go down. All I knew was that an old bomb that had been dormant inside of me for so long could possibly detonate tonight. I thought of Gary scaring the living hell out of Connie and the kid, and that was enough to set me off as I had driven here. She told me that she was in room 201, and I passed the front office with my head hung low. I snuck a peek at the front desk person—he didn't even look up while my dark figure moved through the parking lot.

It was so rowdy in the parking lot with all of the drunken sailors from Norfolk's Naval Base milling around—it was no wonder no one had heard the commotion coming from Connie's room. I knew which room was Connie's as I followed the dropping numbers—the door was ajar, because a pair of her jeans were hanging out of it. I ran to the door and stood to the left of it before cautiously sticking my head in and kicking the jeans inside.

The entire room was in shambles from Gary's tirade. Gary had kept his promise and pinned Connie on the floor with his large body. I slammed the door behind me, but his fury deafened him. His stubby hands were locked tightly around her throat, and he banged her head into the tiled floor over and over. Darren pounded his small fists into Gary's back, but his feeble attempt to protect his mother went unnoticed.

I stalked into the bathroom, grabbed Gary by the collar of his soiled t-shirt and yanked him off of Connie. She gagged and coughed and rolled onto her stomach. Darren knelt at her side crying, while I shoved Gary onto the bed. Surprisingly, the fat bastard bounced back onto his feet in a millisecond.

"You again? You need to mind yo' fuckin' business, white boy! You ain't got no place here!"

"She is my business! I want you to go away and leave Connie the fuck alone!" I shoved him firmly in the shoulder for emphasis. But Gary wasn't going down without a fight. He pulled out a switchblade, and it caught the dull light of the lamp.

"I ain't goin' no damn where. She got somethin' I want, and I ain't leavin' 'til I get it." Gary moved faster than I expected and threw his weight into me. I caught his wrist so that I wouldn't lose sight of the knife, and my back hit the wall. A fake Monet crashed to the floor and shattered at our feet. I regained my footing and used all the strength I had to wrestle the fat fuck to the ground. It seemed like an eternity as Gary and I rolled around on the floor while Connie and Darren watched in silent terror from the bathroom. I made the mistake of letting Gary sit on top of me, and we were both short of breath as I held off his short arm that wielded the knife. I glanced behind Gary as Connie pulled the lamp from its socket.

Gary's eyes followed my own, and he held up his free arm to protect his head. Connie swung the lamp at him with both hands, and Gary cried out when the porcelain shattered against his temple. The knife fell from his hand. Gary smothered me with his body to avoid Connie's wrath.

I dug my knee into his gut and caught a glimpse of Connie with Gary's knife in her hand. She held it high above her head. The blade came down with lightning speed, and I heard the instant sound of ripping flesh. Gary's eyes grew into two discs of surprise.

"Aaargh!" he cried.

Connie stabbed him two, three, four times with the look on her face of a kid who had just eaten a candy bar. Blood shot up everywhere like a decorative fountain. Gary let out a slow groan before collapsing and moments later, a warm, sticky wetness seeped over my chest. I gave Gary a strong push, and he flipped over onto his back. I blinked twice when I saw the knife that dripped in Connie's hand. Connie dropped it and watched Gary's lifeless body as though he would get up and try to strangle her again. Gary's eyes stared up at the ceiling, and I could see all of his rotted teeth in that open mouth. Darren peeked out the bathroom door and Connie blinked as though she had forgotten where we were. She hurried to hide her son's view.

"Darren, baby, I want you to go into the bathroom, lock the door, and don't come out until Mommy tells you to. Okay?"

Darren nodded his head and did as he was told. Once we heard the soft click of the lock, Connie panicked.

"Oh my God, Chris. Oh my God—is he dead?" I ran two hands through my hair and knelt over Gary's face. "Is he?"

"Connie, shut up! I can't tell . . ." But I knew. We both did.

His eyes never shifted, and he had said a thousand words with no sound from that cavern in the middle of his face. "He's not breathing. Oh shit! What are we gonna do?"

"Calm the hell down, Connie! We have to call the police."

"No! You cannot do that!"

"The hell I can't! What the fuck is wrong with you?"

"They're gonna ask too many questions. He's fucking dead, Chris!"

"Don't you think I know that? We'll just say it was self-defense. You saw it, Darren saw it."

"I can't get my baby involved with that."

"We have to, Connie, there's no other way. You just killed somebody. It was self-defense, but you just killed somebody. We have to call the police." I headed towards the phone, and Connie darted across the room and snatched it from the jack.

"Chris, please don't. If Ahmad finds out what happened tonight, he's going to try and take Darren from me."

"No, he won't Connie. We'll explain what happened. Now give me the phone."

"You don't know him, Chris. He's been looking for a reason for a long time. Ever since he found out I was stripping." She held the phone behind her back. "Please, Chris, don't let him take my baby away." I shook my head in disbelief.

"Connie, what do you expect me to do? Get rid of the body?" She returned my wide-eyed stare with defiance. I backed away and squinted my eyes at her. "Are you out of your fucking mind?"

"He's dead, Chris. Think about the questions they're going to ask us. Like why the hell were you here in the first place? Who am I to you? I'm sure your wife's going to wonder the same thing." I sat on the edge of the bed and placed my forehead in my palm. She was naming all of the things I hadn't even thought about. The police would probably charge me with being an accomplice.

And what would I tell Sylvia? That Connie was an old friend I was trying to protect? As if she would believe that shit. I would lose my respect, my business and my marriage, and I would get a chance to think about all of those things in my prison cell.

I felt afraid and helpless, and I didn't like either of the two. My dinner tossed and turned in my stomach at the sight of a dead man lying at my side. Even a man I despised. A man who gazed aimlessly at the ceiling.

"Both of us have too much to lose. Even if Ahmad finds out what Gary has been doing to me all these years, he won't accept a married man coming to my defense. He'll do everything in his power to keep Darren away from me, and I can't let that happen."

"So what are we supposed to do, Connie?" She swallowed hard as though preparing herself for what she was about to say.

"I think you already came up with something."

"Get rid of the body," I whispered to no one in particular.

Chapter 24

Gary was already large, but his dead weight was a much bigger issue. Thank God he wore a dark-colored shirt and pants—the maroon splotches wouldn't be obvious to a passerby. I was glad I left my jacket in the car, because my t-shirt was ruined, and I needed to put on something else. I went into the bathroom and scrubbed my torso, stiff with Gary's dried blood.

I exited the room wondering if anyone could see the fear and guilt stamped all over my face. But no one paid me any attention and probably mistook me for one of the other drunks walking around with nothing covering their upper bodies. I put the jacket on once I reached the car and went back to help Connie. She instructed Darren not to let anyone in while she and I were out of the room.

We had already decided that if anyone studied us just a little too hard, we would say that we were helping a drunken friend to the car who had had one too many. Gary's head drooped over one of his shoulders and rolled left to right as we huffed and puffed across the parking lot. It would have been easier to bring the car around to Connie's room, but we couldn't afford to attract any attention with the crime we were about to commit. I directed her to the secluded area of the car.

I popped the trunk, looked around, and we dropped Gary in there. The car bounced once, and I closed the door of the trunk on that frozen stare. I sped out of the parking lot and listened as Connie told me where we could dump him. I only heard half of what she was saying, thinking of how surreal it was that she was actually calm about all this now. I thought back to what Vince had said to me earlier. *You just watch that one, okay? She's been through some shit.*

Gary had probably scarred her for life, and she did have some issues to deal with. She had said before that he had taught her how to become harder and colder. I had questioned myself over and over ever since she and I started seeing each other, wondering what the hell it was I doing since I had never cheated before.

I never answered that question, I simply continued my actions. But I would never ask myself that again, because I knew the answer.

I let my little head fool the bigger one, and look where it had gotten me. After tonight, I was going to cut Connie off. Seriously this time. I didn't realize how much I loved Sylvia until I found out how far I would go to hide my biggest mistake from her. We coasted down the Campostella Bridge towards the shipyard where the huge military boats sat as emotionless as kings. The barges floating along the Elizabeth River below seemed to be the only form of life in an otherwise dead, summer night. The neighboring industrial buildings were poorly lit stacks of concrete blocks along the shore—perhaps one of their gravelly lots would become Gary's tomb.

At this point, I didn't know where Connie wanted to put him, but I was the first to hear the sirens behind us. It was a sound I had become very familiar with over the past few days.

"Fuck!" I cried. "I cannot believe this shit is happening." If Connie wasn't nervous before, she was now. I could almost smell the sweat at her temples. We both watched as the officer shined the light into the car and approached the driver-side window. I rolled it down and licked my lips.

He fit the role of the stereotypical, donut-eating cop, and his belly rubbed against the car.

"License and registration," he said. He peered into the car and gave Connie a suspicious stare. Her hands were clasped together like she was wringing out a washcloth.

"I'm sorry, officer, but what did I do?"

He gave me a harsh laugh.

"You were doing fifty-five in a thirty-five." Connie handed me the registration from Vince's glove compartment with one of her moist hands. I gave it to the officer along with my license. He looked at the two and then at me.

"They don't seem to match," he said.

"This is my cousin's car. I'm from out of town."

"Obviously. I'll be back." He went to his car, and Connie and I looked at each other.

"Just stay calm, Chris," she whispered.

"You're telling me?" The officer came back to the car and gave me a wary look.

"Tonight, you're lucky. I'm gonna let you go, and that's only because I got bigger fish to fry downtown. Watch your speed."

"Thank you, officer." He gave a stiff nod, and I tried to pull off without speeding again. I really was thankful—he hadn't searched the car. Connie and I could both breathe again, but it wasn't over. We still had a certain gentleman to deal with in the trunk. I drove all the way down the rest of the bridge and made a right onto Kimball Terrace as Connie suggested.

It was a dark street with a slight curve that had a guardrail protecting anyone from careening into the water. Only a couple of minutes away people were drinking, dancing, and eating at the Waterside Mall without a clue that a body was about to be dumped in the Elizabeth River. I parked along the guardrail and turned off the lights. We dragged Gary out of the trunk, aware that at any moment someone could drive around the bend and catch us. It was this fact that gave me the guts to tip him over the side and watch him bob out until he could no longer be seen.

Chapter 25

Connie and I scrubbed the floor of the hotel room for what seemed like hours and picked up the remnants of my fight with Gary. We would just have to replace what had been broken. Darren had either obeyed Connie's words or never left the bathroom because he was too afraid.

I was concerned that the four-year-old would never forget what he had seen tonight. I knew this thirty-six-year old wouldn't. Connie and I knew that people would start asking questions once Gary didn't show up to work on Monday—she said he never missed work, because he loved money too much. We devised a plan that we hoped covered our tracks. I wasn't a professional criminal, so all I could do was pray that it was believable. Gary was a serious gambler, and Connie told me that he had had troubles with loan sharks before—they had come to Gary's house, threatened his life, and made him strip naked in the yard while his neighbors watched. Although it had scared her shitless at the time, Connie was grateful now, because people would be able to vouch for her story.

We went to her home and turned it upside down as though they had come looking for Gary to repay a debt. Connie wasn't going to keep the room after all but would go home on Monday and call the police that morning to report "the break-in" and her uncle missing. She would say that she had stayed over a friend's place for the weekend so she wouldn't have to be home alone—one of the girls at the club owed her a favor and wouldn't have a problem covering for her with no questions asked.

Furthermore, she would deny having seen or heard from Gary since he prepared to leave for his weekend of gambling. She would say that she feared his life may be in danger. That he had complained to her about someone watching him on his way home from the bus stop the past couple of weeks.

Monday. Until then, I would wait.

I didn't stop once on my way home. Vince never questioned my silence before I left, assuming that my past week's troubles were bothering me. My easygoing cousin would probably kill me if he knew that I had transported a body in his car not too long ago. But he would never find out, because I had cleaned it as thoroughly as a hospital room. I told Connie to call me first thing after she had spoken to the police.

$$$$

It was three a.m. when I pulled up in front of my house, and had I not been so tired, I would have run up the driveway. But all of my lights were on, and I knew that something wasn't right here either. I set down my bags in the marble foyer and climbed the stairs to our room. Sylvia was nestled underneath a thin satin comforter, and her hair fanned out over her pillow.

My chest tightened when I saw her and thought about what I had become in just a few days. *What the fuck is wrong with you*, I thought, slamming my fist into the wall. Sylvia sat up and looked at me like a deer caught in headlights. When she saw that it was me, she visibly relaxed and gave me a surprised smile.

"What are you doing back so soon?" She jumped out of the bed and ran to me with open arms. I hugged her tightly.

"Missing you."

"Really, Chris. I mean, I'm happy that you're here, but I wasn't expecting you so soon."

"Then it doesn't sound like you're happy," I teased. She bit her bottom lip.

"I was just hoping that I could speak to you before you came home."

"Why, did something happen? And why are all the lights on?"

"That's what I wanted to speak to you about. My mom is here." I wrinkled my brow.

"She's here now? Visiting, right?"

"Well, she might be staying here for a couple days, just until—"

"Sylvia, not again. You know how your mother is with me."

This wouldn't be the first time Elaine had had one of her episodes in the company of her husband and come to stay with us. Aldo was a very proud man, and he tried to keep Elaine's illness hidden from all of his rich friends.

Whenever they were present, and she started going off on one of her tangents, Aldo would ban her from the house shortly after. He would later tell them that Elaine was taking a vacation, but it was no vacation for me when she came running to my house. Why, I didn't know, since she and I hated each other, and she could have stayed with either of her two sisters in the area. Now, I could see why Sylvia had been so sugary sweet the last time I had spoken to her. She was trying to prepare me for this.

"Baby, you know about mom's problems. She could really use my support right now. I know you two don't get along, but could you give it a try for me?" Sylvia cast her cat eyes up at mine, and I softened like I hadn't with her for quite a while.

"Alright. But it's not going to be for a month like it was last time. I hope you understand that. I hope she understands that, too."

"Just a couple days, I promise." I felt sorry for the broad, what can I say? She was one uppity bitch, but she was still my wife's mother and did have a mental illness. That didn't mean I was going to put up with her bullshit in my own house. Hopefully, I would drive her even crazier than she already was, and then, she would go the hell home. Arguing with her husband would seem like Disneyland in comparison to putting up with me. I kissed Sylvia on her forehead and told her that I would come to bed soon. I walked down the staircase and flipped off a light switch—my mother-in-law and saving electricity were the least of my worries though. As I passed the mirror in the foyer, all I could see was the blood of a certain black man on my face.

My heart raced, thinking of the phone call I would receive from Connie after she had contacted the police. God forbid I get a personal visit from them, an officer coming to throw me in jail like the criminal I was.

I had really done some HBO, Soprano-type shit tonight, and I was always the first one to say that all Italians aren't the way they're depicted on the show. The irony of the situation was that for the first time in a long while, Sylvia had looked at me like she wanted to make love—I couldn't bare to touch her with my dirty hands.

$$$$

I went into my study and placed my hands down on the oak desk. I shook my head to forget the smell of my sweat, Gary's blood, and the water of the Elizabeth River. I noticed a slow movement out of the corner of my eye. The dark silhouette seated in my leather chair let out a soft sigh. I turned on the lamp, and Elaine tilted her head to the side so that her honey-blonde hair swept across her face. She was already drunk—that much was clear from the way her head bobbed up and down. When she looked up again, she gazed at me in such a way that I wanted to back out of the room from a vague discomfort. I grimaced, wondering why she had decided to enjoy a glass of my expensive cognac in a place I escaped to for privacy. She wasn't even supposed to be drinking while taking her medication.

"Wait," she said, barely above a whisper. I wondered if she had used that same voice to catch her husband. Elaine was a beautiful woman for fifty-six, I would give her that. Her olive-colored skin looked like mine, like she was right off the boat. The green eyes that she had given Sylvia were surrounded by tight, glowing skin. She hadn't been spared the healthy breasts or hips either, and one could fit a wedding band around her waist.

I knew all of these things weren't enough for Aldo, though. As attractive as Elaine was, status was everything to her husband since he had been born rich. Elaine wasn't aware of it, but Sylvia had told me that her mother wasn't born with a silver spoon.

Elaine had some nerve judging me when her mother had scrubbed floors for a living, even the floors of Aldo's parent's mansion. He had only intended to screw the pretty daughter of the help.

When she got pregnant, his pissed off parents told him to take care of his business. To live up to his good name, he had turned her into the stuck-up broad she was today. The classy, socialite wife with a wealthy background she and her husband made up. Sylvia made me swear that I would never bring it up around Elaine, but those times that she turned her nose up at me, that's all I wanted to do. Why she wanted me to stay around and chat now was a mystery and a surprise.

"Tell me about your father, Chris." I should have known she would try and make me angry. She knew I didn't talk about my father much and why.

"Elaine, I think you have had too much to drink. Since when have we ever sat down and shared an intimate conversation? We don't care for each other, that's no secret. And why the hell do you want to talk about my father?"

"I have let Aldo rule over me for so long . . . never had a man in my life before him," she slurred. "Nope, no man."

"What are you talking about?"

"I was so young when we met. Didn't know what to look for in a man, but I knew, just knew he had to be it. I didn't have a father to ask for advice. If I did, I probably wouldn't be married to the asshole." My eyes widened and she giggled and hiccupped at the same time. I had never heard her dare speak of her husband in such a way. He was a ruthless, powerful man who was prone to getting things his way, and that was why Sylvia couldn't live under her father's roof. She could never seem to make the right grades, choose the best career path, or even wear the right clothes for her father.

I had freed her from the cell she lived in when we married and accepted her for the great woman she was. Elaine had always defended her husband until now. I didn't want to speak with her further.

"Elaine, I think you need to go to bed." Already, I wanted to call Connie and find out if anything had happened since I left. I knew I was being anxious, and it was too soon.

"I never knew my father, you know," she continued. "My mother didn't speak much about him either. He left us. I want to know what it was like."

"You want to know what what was like, Elaine?" She was beginning to annoy me with this newfound interest in my family tree. "My father was a fucking drunk. There isn't a fairy tale to tell."

"There must have been some good times."

"I guess," I said hesitantly. "Dad was supposed to go pro in football right out of high school. Then he hurt his knee." I didn't add that he had taken it out on my mother on a daily basis. "One time he took me to a Jets game when I was about seven. He promised to get at least one of the players to sign my football before we left, because he said he knew some of them."

I laughed as I reminisced.

"It turns out he didn't know any of them but tried to get me that autograph anyway. He left me with my mom and came back with a signed football. Years later, I found out that he had actually signed it, but I didn't care, because I knew he didn't want to disappoint me."

Elaine hung on to every word I said and crossed her long legs when I was done. Her toned, upper thighs were now visible under her Oriental robe. She made no effort to cover herself. She leaned back in my chair and her nipples poked through the fabric. I cleared my throat and decided that she could stay in my study with the demons that danced around her.

"Goodnight, Elaine."

"Thanks, Chris, but you don't have to leave. I'm going to bed." She called me Chris, and she was being cordial? She was very drunk. Elaine placed her lipstick-stained glass on my desk. She came towards the door and stopped once she reached me, placing a small hand on my shoulder. "Sylvia is lucky to have a man like you."

Elaine kissed me softly on the cheek and closed the door behind her. That was definitely over the top. Elaine had never complimented or touched me. It was more than the alcohol now.

She was definitely up to something. I hoped she didn't think she was buying herself a longer stay.

For now, I didn't have time to figure it out. I couldn't wait until Monday. I needed to call Connie. I dialed the number to Connie's house, since it was easier to remember than her cell, before I realized she was still staying at the hotel. Plus, the police might check Gary's phone records, and my number would surely pop up. My hands began to sweat as I placed the phone back on its cradle. I realized that I had already called Connie at home several times. What if they linked the two of us? The room began to spin, and I sank down into my leather chair that was still warm from Elaine's ass.

Chapter 26

I did end up making love to my wife that night—she was elated after I told her I decided to sell the restaurant in Virginia. It was one of those secrets I added to the list I would die with. I knew why I wanted to touch her. Partly to get away from the things that rattled my brain, but mostly, because I wanted to. She called my name and evoked a burning inside of me that I had forgotten was still there.

I wished silently that it had always been like that, with me inside of her and not Connie. The next day, I cooked for Sylvia, took her for a drive, and we blessed the backseat on the way home.

I decided to get back to my other baby—my restaurant. I had already called my talented chef, Carla Russo, and told her that I was planning a romantic dinner with my wife after hours that evening. Carla made a delicious manicotti, and the way I planned

on decorating the place was bound to knock Sylvia off of her feet. I hoped to knock some of the cheating guilt out of my system, too.

$$$$

I left my house and headed to Balducci's. I made a right turn onto Richmond Avenue, passing all of the small businesses that had lasted through the years. I passed the Staten Island Mall, and already, I could see the cars flooding my restaurant's parking lot—it was business as usual. When I walked into my restaurant, my eyes shined with pride, and I forgot about my troubles for a short time.

Some of my regular customers greeted me, and I gave the place a once over to make sure everything was how I left it. Balducci's was my bread and butter—no pun intended. It always reminded me of how far I had come. Ma would've been happy if she were still here and Dad, too, if he hadn't lost his mind after her death.

Of course, I said I forgot about my troubles for a short time, because everything before me was everything I stood to lose. Every detail I had stressed over—the black marble floors, an indoor pond with exotic fish, booths ensconced with black silk curtains—would all be taken from me if the police discovered what Connie and I had done. I was getting so tired of this "Connie and I" shit. Since when had we become a pair? *A murder keeps you two in unholy matrimony*, said a tiny voice in my head. I jumped at the feathery touch on my back.

"Whoa, are you alright, boss?" Carla said, giving me a funny smile. "I just wanted to show you the new menus and welcome your ass back. You would think I came up behind you with a gun." As though having one drawn at my head wasn't enough.

I had to remember to maintain my cool, to act as though all was well. My employees were used to me running a tight ship, not some nervous man looking over his shoulders every moment. I hadn't felt this panicky since I saw the remnants of my mother blowing her brains out years ago. I wasn't in a rush to become familiar with the sentiment again. I forced a smile and took the new menu from Carla's hand.

"This looks great. How's everything going?"

"Fine. Bobby was having a fit last night, because some hotshot food critic decided to stop by. You know how particular he is."

Bobby was the general manager. He was very high strung, and a few times, his pretty boy lover would stop by my place to tell him so—I promptly put that shit to an end. Besides that, he was a perfectionist, and I knew I could trust him completely with the restaurant. "On top of that, some business contact kept your office phone ringing all morning. Between running to handle your calls and running this place, he pulled what little of his hair he has out. We got some new kid working the kitchen, so I have to get back."

"Did he complain to you about who kept calling?"

Carla walked back towards the kitchen when she turned to me. She looked skyward to remember.

"Christine? No . . . Constance! That's it."

Chapter 27

"Hey, baby," came the husky voice on the other line. After I went over the numbers of the past week with Bobby, I rushed to a gas station just around the corner to call Connie from a payphone. It was neurotic, but I couldn't afford to be sloppy anymore. I figured if she had called me several times after I had just made it into town, then she must have some bad news.

"Connie, what happened?" My heart was so high in my throat that it changed my voice.

"Why do you sound like that, Chris?"

"One of my employees said you called the restaurant several times. Is something wrong?"

"Yes."

"Well, what is it?" I wiped my brow with the back of my blazer sleeve.

"I can't stop thinking about it, Chris."

"Well, it hasn't been easy for me either, Connie."

"It just keeps sending chills up and down my spine."

"You just have to maintain your cool, Connie. If the police notice anything—"

"The police?"

"Yeah, isn't that what you were calling me about?"

"Chris, I was referring to us."

"What about us?"

"I can't stop thinking about you, silly." She giggled softly, and I looked at the phone in my hand. I gritted my teeth and fought the urge to slam the damned thing down in its cradle. She was still talking when I brought it back to my ear. "The last time we touched, you sent chills up and down my spine."

"That should be the last thing on your mind considering—" I stopped abruptly as I watched the number of people walking back and forth past me. Some had even stopped to stare, and I realized that my temper was beginning to show.

How dare she bring up sex at a time like this?

Especially when I thought my phone was ringing off the hook because both of our lives were hanging in the balance?

I didn't even think that I would reach her, because she would already be in a cell, and they would be coming to get me next.

"Connie, I want you to call me back after you call the police on Monday morning like we decided to do."

"I never said I wasn't going to call you before then. Obviously, I couldn't call you at home."

"So you call my place of business? Enough times for the chef to remember your damned name?"

"I'm sorry, Chris, but I didn't think it would be this hard."

"You're only making it that way."

"Why, because I can't forget your face? Or the way you smelled after we made love? Don't you remember any of that?" I closed my eyes for a long time and turned away from the crowd.

"Connie, we killed a man." It was a tortured whisper.

"We killed an animal." There was that iciness again. I didn't like when she talked like that. Like the night she confronted Sylvia's friend at the club. This person was hardly the girl I drank milkshakes with or who cried over me the night after the arson.

"You have to get that way of thinking out of your head if you expect the police to believe you're worried about his whereabouts."

"I will. But in the meantime, I wanted to thank you. I never really got a chance to do so that night."

"Connie, I'm not proud of what we did. It was a senseless accident."

"It was no accident."

"I was defending you . . . and you defended me."

"I wanted to thank you for helping me get rid of him." I didn't know if it was the mugginess outside or what I was starting to believe she was telling me that was making everything spin.

"What . . . what are you talking about?"

"Gary wasn't there by accident." I could hear her smiling from several hundred miles away. "And no one told him where I was staying. No one except me." Connie's words became a faint buzzing in my ear. "He wasn't coming after my sweet ass this time. He was coming after something he loves even more—his money. He had just cashed his check and was ready to go to the damned tracks, but I told him to run up to the corner store and get us some Coronas so we could have a little fun before he left. I took the money from his dresser when he stepped out. I left and used some of it to eat at Friendly's and called him from the restaurant to tell him what I had done. He went ballistic. I told that mothafucka to come and get me. It was perfect."

I was beginning to feel sick. *She got somethin' I want, and I ain't leavin' 'til I get it.* Gary wasn't trying to rape Connie, he just wanted his gambling money back. Connie knew we would get into it once I got there. She had used me. She had used me to help her get rid of him. Permanently.

"I knew as soon as you helped me that you cared about me as much as I cared about you."

"I have to go, Connie."

"Chris, don't feel bad. You knew what he was doing to me and you stopped it."

"I have to go Connie."

"Chris . . . I love you. I know now isn't the time for you to say it back—"

"I said I have to go, goddammit!" I slammed the phone down and jumped into my car.

She was insane.

Now, I began to understand what I had gotten myself into. She had tricked me into this, and there was no turning back. The whole time Connie told me she loved me, I wanted to tell her how much I hated her for incriminating me.

Somehow, I had to swallow a candlelit dinner along with that revelation of the day.

Chapter 28

The dress Sylvia opted to wear was one of my favorites, and she knew it. The emerald green clung to each of her curves and she looked like the precious gem that she was. My acting was brilliant. Under any other circumstances, I wouldn't have had to put on a show, because we hadn't had a romantic moment like this for a while. But a part of my mind was elsewhere, and I didn't want to ruin the night. Rather, I didn't want Connie to ruin the night.

The phone rang like crazy before Sylvia had met me here, and I already had thirteen messages. Undoubtedly, it was Connie trying to finish our previous conversation. But I had no words for her. I didn't plan on speaking with Connie again until Monday. Sylvia and I gently clicked our wine glasses together in a silent toast.

"I'm worried about Mom, Chris," she started. Another person I didn't care to mention. I never did tell Sylvia about her mother's awkward behavior towards me.

Talk about ruining the moment. "She's been focusing on her father too much."

"I would think that would be normal. She never knew him."

"Well, she seems to think that if she had, she would have picked a better man than Dad. That she would have had some guidance in that department."

"He left her as a child. He couldn't have given too much guidance."

"I don't think that's completely true. She seems to believe that her mother may not have wanted her father in her life."

"Why not?"

"I don't know, Chris. But I do think that this thing is bigger than what I originally thought. Maybe if she could find her father, it might take a load off of her depression. After all, that's what's putting the most strain on her marriage accompanied by my father's asshole disorder—"

"Don't tell me you're going to go looking for some guy you or your mother never met."

"Not just some guy, Chris—my grandfather. Mom is only getting worse, and you and I seem to be getting back on track. I want us to be able to have our home to ourselves, and I want Mom to put her past behind her so that she can focus on getting better. That's why I want to search for him." She did have a point. Elaine could finally meet her father, move the fuck on, go home to her husband, and Sylvia and I could continue with our honeymoon phase.

"It seems like that's what Elaine wants, so I think that would be a great idea. But I'm going to be there to help you every step of the way. You don't know what this guy—I mean your grandfather—is like.

"I would really appreciate that, babe."

"Wait a minute, Vee . . . just last night, you were practically begging me to get along with your mother, because she might be staying with us for a little while. Now you seem like you're in a hurry to move her out. What's going on?" Sylvia looked down at her lap and clasped her hands together on the table. She reached across and took one of mine. When she looked up at me, her eyes were bright with tears.

"I'm pregnant." My stomach did a somersault. "You can't expect a new mother to be stressed out already, can you?" I was so happy I didn't know what else to do besides grab her face and kiss her.

"You're pregnant?" This might actually be the first time that Sylvia would see me cry. I came over to her side of the booth. I placed a hand delicately over her stomach. "When did you find out?"

"This morning, after you left for the restaurant. I was nauseated for the past two weeks, but I didn't want to alarm you without finding out for sure. I took the test today, and now, I know."

"A baby. We are having a baby."

"Yes, your baby is having a baby. And there's something else I wanted to talk to you about. I want to go back to work, Chris." I wrinkled my brow and shook my head.

"There's no need for you to go back to work, Sylvia. I make more than enough money to take care of a family."

"It's not that, Chris. I'm bored, and I really miss what I do."

"Working for an asshole lawyer?"

"It was a challenge for me, Chris. Maybe I didn't live up to my dad's expectations of me actually becoming a lawyer, but I ended up working with a district attorney that no one else could handle."

"I told you that I would take care of you. That no wife of mine would ever live uncomfortably. Besides, you're pregnant now. You picked a fine time to want to return to work."

"It's not like I'll be working the whole nine months. Just until—"

"I said no, Sylvia! Talk about stress. You just relax, and let me take care of you like I said I would. And you can take care of that baby inside you."

She wasn't stubborn this time and nodded her head with a sad smile, but I knew she would get over it and see that it was the best thing for our new family. I would be a terrific father, and there wouldn't be any mistakes this time around. I lifted her onto the table and kissed away her uncertainties. It only took one tug of her cocktail dress and a few on my belt to find my way inside of her. Our moans were enough to drown out the urgent ring of the phone that had started up again.

Chapter 29

"**Don't you get** the fucking picture?" I barked into the phone in my study downstairs. Connie actually had the audacity to call my house. Thank God Sylvia and Elaine had decided to visit the city for a few hours of shopping. Elaine had a bad habit of answering my phone and Sylvia—

"Why are you acting like this?"

"I don't have time to play games with you, Connie!"

"You didn't mind playing with me before!"

"That was before I found out what you were really like. I enjoyed the attention, but now, I'm fucking paying for it. Getting involved with you was probably the biggest mistake I ever made in my life."

"It wasn't a mistake when you told me you wanted to make love to me. Or when you came to my rescue in the middle of the night, because the person I hated the most was trying to attack me."

"You lied, Connie!" I shouted. "And you killed a man with my help."

"He deserved it," was her venomous reply. "I *thank* you for it."

"You really need to stop saying that, Connie. I'm hanging up now."

"Wait! I called 911 this morning like you asked me to."

Was it already the beginning of the week? My mind had been in so many places over the last two days that I nearly lost it. I steadied my voice so that she couldn't detect how nervous I was.

"Go on."

"I told the police the story, just like we had planned. They searched the place from top to bottom, and I cried and all that. As hard as it was for me to drop one tear for that sonofabitch, I did. They told me they would do everything in their power to find him."

"So they bought it?"

"Of course they did," she said proudly. My stomach flipped again when she told me that, as though we hadn't a care in the world. "Gary is a well-known gambler. He's had more than his share of trouble with the wrong sort of people. We probably did them a favor. Did I tell you I found a job?"

"It's over, Connie."

"I'm gonna be working at Nordstroms in the mall at a perfume booth. Not as much money, but it's a job."

"Did you hear me? I said it's over."

"I know. They believed me. You don't have anything to worry about."

"I mean all of it. These phone calls, any communication between us *whatsoever*. It's too risky, and I don't have much to say to you anymore."

"But I love you, Chris. And I know you feel something for me."

"The only thing I feel for you now is pity."

"Ha! You, pity me? You, the man who remains in his phony ass marriage with a wife who won't fuck him? A man who's too weak to handle what's staring him right in the fucking face?"

"My wife has seen more of this dick in the last two days than you've seen in your lifetime, sweetheart. And that's a lot of dick. We are beyond happy right now, and I won't let anything or anyone fuck that up."

"Too late."

Connie hung up the phone before I could respond. It was a good thing she did too, because Sylvia came prancing through the door a few seconds later with my mother-in-law at her heels. My wife began pulling pink baby blankets and other infant paraphernalia from her shopping bags. "Don't you think it's a bit early to shop for the baby, sweetheart? We don't even know if it's going to be a girl yet." Sylvia squealed with excitement.

"I know baby, I just couldn't wait. Mom got me all worked up." Elaine plopped down in my chair as she had the other night and crossed her long legs.

"It's never too early to start making decisions for a baby," she said snidely. "I'm sure you're not familiar with that considering your upbringing." I realized that Super Bitch was back, and Sylvia stepped in between the two of us to discourage the tension that was bound to mount. I liked her better when she was drunk. I bit my tongue and smiled at my wife.

"Sylvia, I need to speak with you. Privately." I shot a look at Elaine, and with her head held high, she left the two of us alone in the room. "She's gotta go."

"Don't let her get to you, Chris. She's just going through her mood swings."

"You have always made excuses for Elaine, Sylvia. I think you just need to come to the conclusion that your mother doesn't like me."

"Don't say that, Chris."

"It's true. She doesn't think I'm good enough for you. Never has."

"Well, I did something that might just make her happier than she's ever been. I stopped by my Dad's this morning before we went shopping, and I opened her safe."

"You sneaky thing. How did you figure out the combination?"

"I'm their only child—I came to the conclusion that it must be my birthday, and I was right."

"So what did you find out?"

"Well, I found my mom's birth certificate. My grandfather's name is Jonathan Dollar."

"That doesn't sound Italian."

"I know, but I'm pretty certain this is the right guy. I called a private investigator named Jerry who I've worked with a few times at the D.A.'s office. He's really good. I think we just might be able to find Mr. Dollar, if he's still alive that is."

My wife went on and on about finding her maternal grandfather. All I could think about was Connie's subtle threat and her hanging up in my ear.

The soft click of the phone had sounded as menacing as the cock of a gun.

Chapter 30

"Your mother is dead, son," the sergeant said, his soft brown eyes just meeting my trembling bottom lip. A grown man couldn't even look at me. My eyes had become wild, and the words coming out of my mouth were gibberish—the sentences made as little sense to me as what I had just been told. I fell to my knees and slammed my English book onto the porch over and over to drown out the voices that tried to calm me.

Without warning, I bolted through the stream of blue that yelled and held out bulky forearms—they tried to restrain my race to the back where my mother napped. The sergeant's words still hadn't sunk in even after I saw the bloody handprints across the wall. I found out later the wound hadn't killed her immediately . . .

I must have been shouting in my sleep before Sylvia woke me up from my nightmare. The bed sheets were drenched with sweat, and so was I. It was a sign that something very bad was about to happen—I had been having the same nightmare for years and always right before my luck made a turn for the worst. Sylvia pressed her warm breasts against my chest and nuzzled my ear with her nose to console me. She was used to this by now, and I clung to her, because I was grateful and hoped that one day I would never have to see that horrible vision again.

My stomach remained queasy, and my heart was heavy. Sylvia sent a flurry of kisses across my chest to try to capture my attention, but my nerves were worse than usual this time. I couldn't relax. She appeared frustrated, because any other morning, her talents would have worked. I felt guilty about the fleeting thought of this being payback for the many times she denied me affection. Of course, I knew better than anyone that my wife wouldn't give up easily.

She whipped her dark hair back and slithered beneath our comforter. Instantly, she went to work on my dick, lathering it with her saliva. My thighs jerked, then trembled, then tightened in one fierce motion. My head lolled back on the pillow and I shut my eyes. I slid my hands beneath the sea of cotton and found Sylvia's strands of silk.

I bit into my bottom lip so badly that I nearly cut it open and found a steady rhythm with her lips.

Sylvia loved it when I gripped her hair and fucked her mouth. Each time I raised my hips, she swallowed me a little deeper, and my eyes rolled into the back of my head until the whites showed. Something was different about the way she sucked on me. It was almost like listening to a song that didn't have the right melody. I had always enjoyed Sylvia going down on me. In fact, I had never had any complaints. But this morning, she was like a wild animal. It was a little too good, if that's even possible for a man.

I could hear her quiet moans, something she usually did when she knew that she was pleasing me. Suddenly, my eyes snapped wide open and I could feel myself about to cum in her mouth. I snatched the comforter off of her head to watch.

"That's right baby, cum," she said, with my dick still in her mouth. At that moment, she rendered me speechless, because all I could see was Connie's face. She continued to focus on what was below and not my wide-eyed shock. The black silk was gone, and now, the only things hanging in her face were satiny curls. The excitement was a typical male reaction, but the anger was not. The two were mixed into one bittersweet batter.

I sat myself up on the bed and rested my back against the headboard. My fingers became entangled in her hair as my grip tightened on her head. She glanced up with a surprised glint in her eyes but didn't stop. I brought her head down a little harder and lifted my hips to drive myself into her mouth with the same vehemence. She mumbled something that I couldn't make out, yet I quickened my pace with erotic fury.

She squirmed and tugged away from me slightly, her moans turning into high-pitched whimpers. Still, I held onto her. It turned me on even more. I wanted to hurt her. I wanted her to feel that she couldn't get away from the pain I inflicted. I wanted Connie to know that I had the control . . .

The moment she grazed the tip with her bottom teeth, I cried out and fell from my trance. This was not Connie. This was my wife. Sylvia cowered at the end of the bed and studied me as though we had never met. It wasn't the look a woman gives a man when she can't wait to get him into bed either. She looked at me as though I was a stranger, like my eyes had lingered on her tits for too long as we passed each other on an empty street. The room was suddenly quiet and icy and I longed for one of us to say something or even start yelling to break the rigid silence.

"Chris," Sylvia began, surprisingly calm, "Is there something you want to tell me?" Oh my God, I thought, she knows I cheated. I sighed deeply, preparing myself for the confession. I opened my mouth to reveal what I had done, almost relieved that I could relinquish the secret even if it was to my own wife. I was tired of the hiding and the guilt. Although I had no intention of telling her what I had done to Gary, I thought that this would at least take some of the burden off of my weary shoulders. But Sylvia raised her hand for me to wait. She wasn't finished.

"Maybe you should talk to someone about it." I frowned, thinking that maybe she and I weren't on the same page. "These nightmares are making you crazy . . . I mean, I've never seen you get that . . .

that rough with me." The truth caught in my throat—I wanted to spit it up so badly that I nearly gagged on it. Sylvia had unknowingly given me a scapegoat, a reason to be a coward. Forcing the truth out of me and asking it of me were two very different things. I knew before I even uttered a word I was going to take the easy way out.

"I . . . I can't seem to shake this dream about my mother's suicide." That wasn't a lie, but it wasn't the real reason I had went sadomasochistic on my wife. When I struck Sylvia in the face before my business trip, she had retaliated with anger. But she also knew that I was upset about the comment she made towards my mother. This time, there was no logical reason for my sudden anger, at least not one I could give her—I ended up looking like a psycho.

"Seriously, Chris, maybe you should see a doctor—"

"No. I'm not going to pay some shrink five hundred dollars an hour to talk to me about my feelings." I was being a little bitch again because I didn't want someone picking my brain, revealing why my head was so fucked up. I was finally at a point in my life where I lived confidently, successfully. I didn't want to share the lowest points of my beginnings with anyone, not even myself.

Yeah, I would begin as I lay on the doctor's couch, *my father made my mother bruise or bleed every day, depending upon which one he wanted to see. She always came up with a different excuse when I came home from school like falling on the porch steps with groceries or running into a table. Eventually, my father didn't care if I saw them arguing or the drunken beatings, and she couldn't hide it anymore.*

All I could do was lock my bedroom door behind me and pray that she would stop crying and that maybe, just maybe, the belt buckle would break across her back like it did last time so that he would stop. I would also pray that God would make me man enough to stand up to my father one day so I could stop the beatings and save her. He didn't answer that prayer until after she was dead—at least the part about me becoming a man . . .

"Chris, please—"

"I'll think about it."

"But—"

"I'll think about it."

Sylvia, unsure of what I might do next, went to her armoire and quickly slipped on a pair of pink pajamas. She turned on her side, and soon, I could hear her snoring softly.

I slipped on my robe and went to call the woman with the wine of temptation dripping from her lips—she had left me drowning in a pool of madness.

Chapter 31

"Connie?" I whispered. I glanced around nervously even though I had locked myself inside my study. It was crazy, but I checked the closet, too.

"Chris, you never cease to amaze me. To what do I owe the pleasure of this call, considering the last one didn't end on such a good note?" I ran a hand through my hair and idly shifted some papers on my desk. I couldn't resist asking the question to which I needed an answer.

"When is this going to stop?" Connie quieted for a moment. I glared at the phone, waiting for a response.

"Well?"

She purposely remained silent, so I placed her on speakerphone and turned down the volume. I lit a cigar and puffed away my impatience and anxiety. Propped my feet up on the desk. Reclined in my chair. Tried to force myself to believe that everything was cool. Still, she said nothing.

"Well?" I said one more time, my voice a little more strained.

"When I say so!" she screamed at the top of her lungs. "Not a moment sooner, not a moment later!" I sat up so quickly that my manila folders and everything in them fell to the floor. I grabbed the receiver and snatched it up.

"Look, just calm down—"

"No, *you* look. It's definitely not going to end sooner because there's somewhere I have to go. And I want you to come with me."

"And where might that be?" I said through clenched teeth. I was furious that I even had to humor her.

"They found the body, Chris." My jaw dropped like a dummy's, and Connie was the ventriloquist. "And you know what that means." My heart skipped a few beats, and the cigar failed to do its trick. Busted. We were going to the police station. For what, questioning?

"No, I don't know what that means, Connie." I hesitated and wondered if I really wanted her to answer my next question. "Do . . . do they think we had anything to do with it?"

Connie began to laugh hysterically, something I think she did when she meant to belittle someone.

"Don't be a dumb ass, Chris. Do you really think I would be this calm if they did?" I couldn't believe she considered her ranting to be calm. I was beginning to think that she was just as bipolar as my mother-in-law, and if that was the case, then I was in for some real trouble. Some of the tension loosened in my muscles when I realized that the police didn't know we were homicidal criminals—at least one of wasn't. But I was still worried about the results of finding Gary's body. Connie rambled on about us not having to worry, and I wasn't really paying attention to her until she finished her last sentence. I didn't think I had heard her correctly.

"What did you say?"

"I said, I want you to attend the funeral with me." I blinked my eyes rapidly.

"Are you crazy?" Connie sighed as though I was a child she was about to discipline.

"Chris, you didn't think I wasn't going to bury my own uncle now, did you?"

I shook my head, unsure of why Connie couldn't understand my disbelief.

"Of course, I expected you to bury him . . . but why do I have to be there to see it?" I was whining now, and I didn't like it. Connie was playing a game with me. She wanted us to be together, and I had brushed her off.

I wished I hadn't been unfaithful at all, but I also wished that the other woman could have at least been sane. Hell, she could have even smashed my car windows before all of this had to happen.

"I don't want to go through this alone, Chris."

"Go through what, Connie? You don't give a damn if the man is dead—you wanted him dead!"

"You're damned right I did!" she hollered. I could hear her heavy breathing over the phone as she began to sob. "I want to make sure he gets put into that ground, and when nobody's looking, I'm going to stand on top of that grave, piss on it, and jump for joy!" Connie sniffed a few times and regained her composure. "I need you here to celebrate with me."

"No, I can't do it. Not for that reason. I can't look at him again."

"That's fine, Chris. The body was a little bloated. It's going to be a closed casket."

"I can't do it, Connie."

"You can't do it?" she replied viciously. "Or you won't?"

"Connie, I don't think it's smart for me to be there," I said, trying a different avenue. "I don't want people questioning who I am and why I came to this man's funeral."

"Look, the funeral's going to be very small. I told you that Gary didn't have much family, and only about two of his high-school friends got in touch with me. So you're fine."

"No, I'm not fine. I can't forget about what we did to him and it's not right for me to be there—it's not right for you to be there!" I could hear Connie tapping her fingers on something like she was trying to maintain her patience with me. It sounded like she was breaking each and every one of my bones.

"Do you remember when we saw your wife's friend in that nightclub?" I did, but I refused to respond. I knew that another threat was about to be issued. "How hard do you think it would be for me to find her?"

"What is your point?" I hissed.

"My point is, do you think she would ever mention that little incident to your wife if she found your number?" I looked at my feet, because I hadn't even thought of it. "Most women would." I knew my wife. She would never stand for adultery—that was the main reason why I was trying so hard to spare her the truth. I knew the marriage would be over if she ever found out. And Karen *had* seen us together . . .

"In New York, Karen won't be that easy to find," I said with an air of uncertainty sprinkled with cockiness. "Besides, you told her we were business connects. I can just as easily tell my wife the same." Of course I knew, like Connie knew, that Karen hadn't believed that story at all. Connie simply hadn't cared.

"How about I call Sylvia and ask her to play catch up with her former co-worker? I'm sure she can get Karen's new number from someone at the D.A.'s office."

"You wouldn't dare."

"I think you know that I would dare. Though it would actually be the truth."

"My wife doesn't need to be brought into this."

"I didn't bring her into it. You did."

Crazy broad. I knew what she wanted to hear.

"I'll go with you to the funeral, Connie," I mumbled.

"Great," was all she said, and she proceeded to tell me about all of the arrangements. I felt like I was supposed to be going to a birthday party.

"I can't stay down there too long, Connie," I said. I wanted to at least keep some of my masculine pride after giving in to her.

"You know we make the best of whatcvcr timc wc havc."

Chapter 32

Sylvia did not disagree with me leaving this time. I told her that I was going on another brief business trip to tie up some loose ends I had left in Virginia. I think she felt like I needed some space, and maybe she did, too, after what happened a few days before.

I sat on an airplane with my face the same mint-green color as the flight attendant's uniform. It wasn't because I was airsick either. I knew that in a few moments, my accomplice would pick me up from the airport only to take me to another unwanted destination tomorrow. I didn't want it to come, yet I couldn't wait to get Gary's funeral over with.

$$$$

"Chris!" Connie cried, waving her hand in the air. The ringlets atop her head were tightly coiled, and her face was glowing. It looked as though she had been sleeping well and hadn't a care in the world. If I looked like walking death,

Connie either didn't notice or didn't mind. Any other day, I would have paid a lot of attention to the jeans that clung to her hips or the off-the-shoulder top that revealed her midriff. But her juvenile appearance didn't excite or fool me. Connie was all woman. She may have been off balance, but she certainly proved that she was ahead of the game by stringing me along on the leash she had placed around my neck.

Connie flung her arms around me and tightened her embrace. I remained as stiff as a board, my arms at my sides. Connie pulled away and gave me a light peck on the mouth.

"I understand if you're still upset with me." I looked around the main entrance of Norfolk International Airport until I allowed my eyes to finally settle on Connie's face again. Her eyes twinkled. Connie's desire for me beat out my despise for her.

"Can you just take me to my hotel room? I'm tired." Connie helped me with one of my small bags and looped our arms together so that she could walk me to her car. Some people smiled at us when they noticed her happy gait—they were completely oblivious to the frown on my face. I sat in the car and rested my face on my palm like an angry child while she drove. Connie spared me the phony conversation after realizing I had no intentions of speaking with her further. Upon dropping me off at the Mariott in downtown Norfolk, Connie leaned over and pressed her lips against my cheek.

"This will all be over after tomorrow . . . we'll be able to put this Gary mess behind us."

For the first time since I had laid my eyes on Connie that day, I smiled. She seemed pleased with this reaction, so I leaned over and pressed my lips to her cheek, too. It was a Judas smile and a Judas kiss. Before the day was over, I was going to do some research of my own. I hoped it would give me the upper hand I so desperately needed.

$$$$

The taxi pulled up in front of Connie's home, and I walked around to the fence surrounding the backyard. I peeked over my shoulder to make sure that no one would ambush me or even report me to the police for what I was about to do. The street was surprisingly quiet, and the corners were empty. My heart pounded, and the sweat rolling down my forehead felt like liquid fire in my eyes. I opened the chain-link fence with no problem and walked to the backdoor of the house.

The eerie melody of wind chimes sounded like a dead man laughing at me. I hesitated. I didn't know if I would be able to handle seeing anything that Gary owned inside the house. Of course, the funeral was tomorrow, so I would have to prepare myself. I was so anxious to get the breaking and entering over with that I almost went about it the sloppy way—I actually thought about breaking the back door window with my elbow.

I had to calm down and start making my decisions logically. It appeared that that was why Connie was ahead of me in the game. I hadn't thought logically since the beginning of this whole mess.

I looked to my feet and rolled my eyes. Why hadn't I thought to look underneath the welcome mat first? I shifted it with my foot and saw the silver shine of a key. I picked it up and looked over my shoulders twice before unlocking the door. When I stepped inside, I wasn't sure if this was the same place I came to when I returned Connie's wallet that day. The place smelled of jasmine and vanilla and the forlorn pictures of Connie that were on the walls had been taken down. She had replaced them with those of her son, parents, and a few other people whom I didn't recognize.

The worn and ratty furniture that had been in the kitchen was no more—only a modern glass table stood there now accompanied by leather seats that looked like they had cost a fortune. If I had been worried about discovering any remnants of Gary, I wasn't anymore.

As I made my way towards the steps, I realized that Connie must have slaved like a dog the last couple of days. There was no way that anyone in the free world would ever know that a fat, disgusting slob like Gary had existed. Boxes were piled into towers along the walls in the upstairs hallway—those must have been more of his things she planned to get rid of. She had been planning all along. I opened the door to her bedroom and instantly dove for her dresser, hoping to find anything that would incriminate her. If Connie was as calculating as she had already proven herself to be, there had to be more information I could dig up on her that would keep her the hell away from me. I found nothing there, so I turned to her closet. Maybe I would find something tucked away up top. My eyes caught sight of a small mahogany chest, and then, I heard tires turning into the driveway.

I dashed over to Connie's window and watched as her Camaro pulled up. She exited the car with a ton of shopping bags. My legs were petrified, and I knew this would get ugly if I didn't move. I ducked to the floor, hoping to shimmy underneath the bed. My large frame wouldn't fit, and I heard the front door slam. She was at the bottom of the staircase now. Damn, she had moved quickly with all of those things in her hand. Her nails tapped against the banister as she climbed . . .

I could hear her voice drifting up the steps while she spoke to someone on her cell phone. Her elated tone would certainly turn sour if she caught me snooping around her room. I took a peek down the hallway through the crack in her door.

Maybe I could move to another room if she hadn't made it upstairs yet.

"Shit," I muttered when I saw her reach the top step. My only other option was to hide in the closet. Stiletto heels click-clacked along the wooden floor as I slid open the closet door, hoping that she couldn't hear its slow creaking. I had just finished trying to close it when Connie walked into the room. The door was still slightly ajar, but maybe Connie would be so caught up in her conversation that she wouldn't notice. My only other fear was that she would have to come inside the closet for anything. I watched her through the slats in the door.

Sweat popped up along my upper lip as Connie kicked off her shoes, rubbed her feet and laughed about something the person must have said on the other end of the phone.

"Yeah," she replied, "We are gonna do a job on Chris tomorrow night." I resisted the urge to jump out of the closet and choke the truth out of her. Do a job on me? With whom? So Gary's funeral wasn't the real reason Connie had asked me to come down here. I should have known she was up to something, but if she thought to do me harm as she had her uncle, she had another thing coming. I wouldn't allow her to kill again.

Connie snapped the phone shut and glanced around the room. She pulled her blouse over her head and unbuttoned her skinny jeans. Connie knelt down to peel the jeans from her immense thighs and raised her head—it seemed like she looked right at me. She frowned. I grabbed at whatever fabric I could to cover myself in that dark space. She came towards the closet, and I took a step back as though I could mesh with the wall behind me. I held my breath when she extended her hand towards the closet door . . .

It turned out that she just wanted to close it. I exhaled softly and wondered how long I had been holding my breath. She finished undressing, snatched a towel from a hook on the bedroom door, and padded down the hall to the bathroom. I could hear her drawing a bath as I pondered when I should make my great escape.

The water stopped running so I slipped out of my hiding place. I quietly opened the bedroom door and crept down the hallway. I had nearly made it to the staircase when the wooden panels creaked beneath my heavy feet.

My heart felt like a boulder trying to force its way through my ribcage—I could hear the wild splashing and sloshing of the tub.

I wasn't sure if she had heard me or not, because the next thing I knew, I was sprinting. I couldn't afford to get caught, I couldn't afford to get into any more trouble.

I never even locked the back door behind me. The grass felt like quicksand around my ankles and the gravel on the street like thumbtacks piercing the soles of my feet. I must have looked like a crazy man running down that street with no destination in sight.

Chapter 33

Connie came to pick me up from the hotel the next morning promptly at eleven. She wore a snug, black seersucker suit and dark sunglasses. I began to believe that black should be her color of choice. The sunglasses were probably used to keep the warm rays from melting her icy eyes. God only knew how cold she would be today as she watched them lower her uncle into the ground.

My own eyes were surrounded by dark circles—I hadn't slept a wink considering I lay awake all night wondering how this day would go. I knew exactly how the evening would pan out though, because Connie wouldn't havc thc chancc to get rid of me. It was hard, but I had made my decision about what I needed to do to get rid of her.

"Constance," I said, giving her a curt nod. She coddled my face with both hands and kissed me squarely on the mouth.

"Let's just put this whole thing behind us, baby," she whispered into my ear.

"We won't have to worry about what we did ever again."

Is that what you'll be saying to someone else about me, bitch? I thought. I wanted so badly to scream at her that I knew what she up to. But I held my tongue and promised myself that I would have the last laugh later on that evening.

$$$$

Connie sat in the front pew of the church with her head hung low. She had walked in the same way and her steps had faltered after seeing the casket. An older black gentleman had gingerly held her by the elbow and guided her to where she now sat with me. I refused to help her—I knew it was all an act. Still, she sat sniffing and dabbing at her eyes while one of Gary's old classmates, Maceo Tatum, spoke at the podium.

Connie watched him with wet eyes while he told some anecdote about him and Gary stealing as kids out of a Mom and Pop store. She couldn't have cared any less than I did. Connie was right about one thing though—there weren't that many people there to see Gary rest in peace.

Or, in his case, rest in anguish. But it also meant there were less people to see through our lies.

To think, beneath that solid oak was a man I had seen take his last breath because of me. My mouth went as dry as the Persian Gulf when I envisioned him opening the coffin, pointing accusingly at me and Connie in a fit of rage. Just when I thought the funeral couldn't get any more ridiculous, the reverend asked Connie if there was anything she wanted to say.

Connie hesitated and gave a small nod. My upper lip curled, and I looked away from her. She slowly walked to the front of the funeral home and gripped both sides of the podium for "support."

"Gary was a great man," she began. She looked down at her hands as if searching for the right words to say—only I knew that she was looking for the safe words to say. "He never asked for much and he was always willing to give. He was the type of person that you always wanted to be around, and he always loved real deep . . . it's too bad that he had to be taken away so soon without showing the rest of the world his special kind of love."

I could have sworn that Connie smirked after that last line, but she tightened her lips and pulled it back in.

$$$$

Connie should have won a Golden Globe for the way she laid it on thick at the gravesite. She sobbed and threw herself on top of Gary's coffin, moaning about how he was her last kin in the world. It made me want to throw up, and eventually, I couldn't take it anymore. I trudged back to the car. I felt horrible thinking about it, but when I had dumped Gary's body into that river, I had had no intentions of seeing him again. Even though the coffin had never been opened, he was still too close for comfort.

Chapter 34

Connie brimmed with mirth as we headed back to my hotel. I could tell by the soft smile that tugged at her lips as she recalled some happy memory in her mind. She let the wind blow through her hair while she drove.

"You know, Gary left me the house."

"Did he?" I asked, uninterested.

"Yes. In fact, someone broke in yesterday." That caught my attention. I shifted uncomfortably in my seat and focused my eyes on a guardrail outside my window. Anything not to have to look at her. "Well, they really didn't break in. Someone found the key under the mat and just let themselves in—who the fuck would be that brave? Only a desperate man, I think." I spun to my left and faced her—I was tired of her goddamned games.

"Are you trying to ask me something? Because I don't like when people beat around the fucking bush with me, Connie."

"Okay, so I'll ask you straight out . . . were you in my house yesterday without my permission?"

"No," I said, my eyes never wavering from her face. She studied me briefly and turned her focus on the road. Connie sighed.

"I don't believe you," she murmured, and mashed her foot down on the accelerator. My body was thrown back and she wove in and out of several cars. I shouted for her to slow down and even attempted to grab the wheel. Connie nudged me with her elbow and continued to pick up speed.

As we headed towards a sharp curve, Connie started to lose control of the car. Suddenly, she hit the brakes, and the Camaro fishtailed on the freeway. A truck horn blared somewhere nearby, and I shut my eyes, waiting to feel the impact of a collision. When I opened them we had come to a stop on the shoulder. Connie patted my knee and gave me a bright smile.

"I was just fucking with you, Chris. I believe you."

"Do you realize that you could have killed us both?" I asked her through clenched teeth. My jaw might as well have been wired shut.

"At least we would have went together," she replied. Connie leaned over and laid her head on my shoulder. Here she was trying to get affectionate with me while people drove by cursing us and flipping us the finger. "Now that the house is all mine, I want you to come over tonight. I thought we could celebrate Gary's homegoing and our reunion." I answered her with an emotionless nod of the head. I would have to be numb to pull off what I had planned for the evening. I didn't want to go through with it again, but I had too.

The fact that she had a child had crossed my mind, but I reasoned with myself that Darren would still have a good father to raise him. There was no sense in him being exposed to an unstable mother. The poor kid had already witnessed a murder because of her.

$$$$

When the taxi dropped me off in front of Connie's house that evening, I dabbed the sweat from my forehead for the fourth time. I tried to steady my quivering hand so that I could ring the doorbell.

Connie swung the door open like a wife happy to see her husband arriving home.

"Come on in," she purred, "I'll meet you in the dining room." She had on an apron that read, *Kiss the Sexy Chef.* A well-done steak, baked macaroni and cheese, and cabbage awaited me at the table. Everything smelled wonderful, but I wasn't sure if she had poisoned it—I was pretty certain that she would have done it to keep me from going home to my real wife. I didn't think that a simple examination with my eyes would do, so I waited for her to return and join me for dinner. She had gone all out with dimly lit candles and undulating music in this otherwise romantic setting. Peaceful moments like these reminded me of how surreal Connie's feelings were towards me.

Connie came back to the table with a pin-striped dress on that looked like a man's oversized dress shirt. She had a belt tucked neatly around her waist. Her open-toed black pumps extended her strong legs. It was a shame what I was going to have to do to such a lovely young girl. But I had to remember what Connie was capable of.

"Aren't you gonna taste my cooking?" she asked, gesturing towards the food before me.

I didn't want to upset her again by telling her I didn't have an appetite for arsenic. "Why don't you come down here for a minute?" I replied. Connie cast her husky eyes up at me.

"Ready for your dessert, huh? You should have told me what you really had a taste for . . ." She walked towards me and dragged her fingertips along the length of the table. I pulled Connie down on my lap, and she repositioned her ass on my groin.

"No," I said. "You cooked all of this for me, and I want to feed you." I got your ass now, I thought. I scooped a forkful of macaroni off of the plate she had prepared for me.

Surprisingly, Connie appeared pleased and opened her mouth. I began to feed her mouthful after mouthful before realizing that maybe she hadn't tampered with my dinner. Now, I was ready for her to get up since she had passed that test, but it turned Connie on that I was pampering her, and she had no intention of moving. Connie slowly and deliberately dragged her wide tongue across her lips.

"You know, you may not be ready for dessert, but I am," she said. She finally stood and adjusted her dress.

"Connie, it's getting late." That was a terrible excuse, because I had just arrived. Connie wagged her finger at me and smiled mischievously.

"Now, now Chris. You can't finish a delicious dinner without dessert. Come upstairs in about five minutes."

Connie went twisting up the steps before I could object further. The air conditioner was pumping, and I was still sweating. I thought I would be ready for this moment, telling myself over and over again that this was the only way out. Now that the opportunity had arisen, all I wanted to do was run out the front door. Of course, that was out of the question. I would certainly face Connie's wrath, and as much as I hated to admit it, I was afraid of her. It had been a long time since I feared anyone, and I didn't like it. I believed at that very moment that any man could succumb to desperation in the face of fear. I was going to kill her, so I guess that made me that man.

Chapter 35

I fingered the butterfly knife that fit snugly in between my waist and my slacks. The pounding in my chest drowned out my footsteps. I approached Connie's room. She hadn't left any lights on, but it wasn't hard to figure out that her room was the one with the door slightly ajar. I followed the eerie orange glow coming from that door and the incense smoke that curled like a beckoning finger.

How am I going to do this? I thought before walking inside. Would I run into the room and leap on top of her? Or would I play it safe and stab her in the back while she wasn't looking? I made up my mind to do it as soon as she turned away from me. I didn't want to see her face when I did it, especially if it looked anything like Gary's had once I was done. I kept one shaky hand at my waist and wiped my brow with the other. I grasped the doorknob tightly, but it slipped out of my sweaty palm. I wasn't ready. I hadn't thought about the consequences of what I might do, because I was so anxious to get rid of Connie. I wanted her out of my life once and for all, but I knew I couldn't live with watching someone die again. I didn't want to feel the warm, sticky blood gushing through my fingers...

To think, I had even come up with an excuse to take a mother away from her child. No matter how much I gave myself the pep talk, I knew there really was no pep talk when it came to murdering someone. I was becoming just as sick as she was.

"Chris?" Connie called out, not knowing I was on the other side of the door. Before I went in her room, I rushed down the hall looking for a bathroom. Once I found one, I went to its tiny window and flung it open. With trembling hands, I took the knife from my belt and threw it out onto the lawn. I slammed the window shut and headed back.

I paused when Connie sat up on the bed. The sheer black teddy she wore left nothing to the imagination. It didn't affect me though—I was used to seeing what Connie was working with. My nerves were so bad at this point—from knowing that I had come close to killing her—that she could have been wearing a garbage bag, and I wouldn't have noticed.

Connie tossed her loose curls about and stretched across the bed. The side of her face lay in the palm of one hand, and she fiddled with a tassel on her teddy with the other. All of a sudden, she raised one of her toned legs at a ninety degree angle and gave me a sexy smile. She ran her fingertips from her ankle to her thigh to the hairless cleft between her legs where she wore no panties. Connie began to do sort of an itsy-bitsy-spider dance with her hand across her clit, teasing herself.

I tore my eyes away from her. The truth of the matter was she was teasing me. She was a damned pro when it came to teasing men. Though now, it was different. She was used to men giving her whatever she wanted because they hoped she would fulfill their sexual needs in return. But she wasn't used to wanting a man on a higher level who denied the temptation she emitted. Of course in the beginning, I had been no different from the other idiots Connie had controlled with her body to get what she wanted. The irony of the situation was that what she wanted from me, I couldn't pull out of my pocket. Still, Connie continued to use what had always worked for her. Even though I tried to keep my focus on the two glasses of Pinot Grigio on her nightstand, my eyes would always wander back to her. "Chris, look at me," Connie whispered hungrily. "Look at me."

Connie lowered her leg and cupped her left breast. She brought it to her lips and flicked her tongue across her own nipple. My bottom lip trembled between the guilt of wanting to suck on it and the irritation of wondering why I wanted to. Connie would clearly do anything to either have me or ruin me, and the concept still didn't stop the blood from rushing to my groin. I was, as she had put it before, a man.

Since Connie always threatened my marriage with what we had done, I felt as though there was something else I should be doing besides allowing her to tempt me. I hadn't come up with a solution yet so it seemed like I was asking for it.

Until I figured everything out, I wouldn't get Connie off my back—as long as she pursued me, she would always be willing to lay on hers. She must have read my mind, because she crawled across her lavender comforter on her hands and knees towards me. She possessed the "fuck me" look all over her dewy face, moist from the perspiration of anticipation.

Connie released a bubbly laugh and asked, "Why are you so nervous, Chris? You act like you ain't seen all this before."

"I'm not," I said coolly, lifting my chin. I had to get myself together. I had seen it all before and then some. It was hard trying to will my own body into obeying me. I compared it to that moment of being half-asleep—the part of my brain that was awake would tell my body to wake up, yet my eyes would remain glued shut. Did I already say I hated not having the control? "I didn't know that I was coming here for this."

Connie grabbed the collar of my shirt and brought her lips about a centimeter from mine.

"You need to relax, Chris. I'm going to make you forget all about your wife. And I'm going to make you remember why you cheated on her in the first place." I looked away from her when reminded why

I was there to begin with. But Connie wasn't having it. She gripped my chin and softly, but firmly, forced me to look at her.

"Have a glass of wine with me. I want you to loosen up. I want you to *want* me, because you know I have a problem with rejection."

The only face I could see was Sylvia's. I couldn't do this. I couldn't fuck Connie and enjoy it, though any man would have called me stupid. I had learned my lesson, but I guess God didn't think I had been taught well enough. Connie leaned across the bed and brought a wineglass to my lips.

"Drink," she ordered.

I gingerly took a sip. *Fuck it*, I thought, before downing the whole glass. I needed to be drunk.

"That's what I'm talking about," she murmured.

I would do what I had to for the night and come up with a better idea to get rid of Connie later. She wouldn't have my heart or my mind, simply my dick. And I hoped that would keep her content for a little while longer.

Connie licked the tartness from my lips and plunged her tongue so deeply in between them that she grazed the roof of my mouth. Suddenly I felt funny, and I knew it wasn't her deep kisses that were doing it. The room wobbled a bit, and then, the wobbling turned into a full-fledged spin. I stumbled to the left, and Connie giggled against my mouth. The firm grip she had on my shoulders tightened.

"Whoa . . . I got you. I didn't know I had that effect on you, baby."

"N . . . no, Connie. I . . . I don't feel right." This time, I stumbled to the right and grabbed the footboard after completely losing my balance. I saw doubles, and my eyes watered. I rubbed them with my knuckles, but they continued to spill over. "Something's wrong . . . wrong with me." I slumped over the footboard and landed on the bed with a bounce. Connie's annoying giggles rang like echoes in my ears. I felt like I was tripping off of something. I *was* tripping off of something. I knew it when I saw the sneaky smile cross her face. She had drugged me.

I had believed that the food was going to kill me, but that would have been too obvious. How could I forget that Connie was used to making things appear to be what they were not? She had used those tricks on me before when I helped her kill Gary. There I was, dying proof that what comes around goes around. I thought I knew what I was walking into, but apparently, I had run into a brick wall again. I would be Connie's next victim in a matter of minutes. Maybe seconds, depending upon what she had given me. I turned over onto my back. The rhythm of my rapid heartbeat would soon slow down. Then stop.

Chapter 36

Connie slapped me twice. I must have blacked out for a moment. I didn't appreciate the slaps, but at least that meant I was still alive. I tried to keep my unsteady gaze on her. She straddled my waist, and her hands were on my chest. Half of her face was hidden by a sinister shadow while the other half switched from shades of blue to red to a bright purple. At least I was only seeing one of her now.

I figured since I was still breathing, there was no better time than the present to bring her with me. I stretched out my feeble arms and attempted to wrap my fingers around her delicate throat. Connie grabbed my hands instead.

"Chris, I didn't give you too much of that stuff, did I?" Now she wanted to tease me. I tried to pull my hands from her grasp but she held on and kissed my fingers. "Say something."

"Trying . . . trying to kill me . . ." I mumbled.

"What?" she asked, leaning her ear towards my mouth.

"How could you poison me?" I asked in a loud whisper. Connie gave me a bewildered look and threw her head back in laughter. She was ruthless. I had how callous she could be after murdering someone, but now, I felt it. I was in Gary's position, and because of that, her "I don't give a damn" attitude turned into "I don't give a fuck."

"Chris, why would I poison you? I wanted to make you feel good, not kill you. I knew that you might have some objections about what was going down tonight, so I put a little something in your drink." She stroked my cheek. "I told you before that I wanted you, Chris. All of you. Now, it's time for your little surprise."

Connie pulled two scarves from underneath one of her pillows and carefully began to tie both of my wrists to the headboard. I made a futile attempt to struggle with her, because I still didn't believe what she had said—I had to be free to escape if she was lying about not wanting to kill me. The fuss I put up only seemed to amuse her further.

She got up and headed towards the door. "I only give my man the best treatment, Chris. Hopefully, you'll have that figured out after tonight."

While Connie was out of the room, I tried to figure out a way to loosen my bound wrists. But she had tied them in a fucking boy scout knot, and there was no way I was getting free. I grew tired, and to pass the time, I simply watched the shadows dance across the walls from the dying candles.

When Connie returned, she didn't come back alone. There was a young woman at her side—she was the color of ground cinnamon and had a short, Halle Berry cut. They were hand in hand, both with mischievous smiles on their faces. I swallowed hard when it became clear to me what Connie's little surprise was.

"Chris, I want you to meet my friend, Vanessa. She doesn't say much, but then again, that's not why she's here." Connie turned to her "friend" and pecked her on the mouth. "I want you to take real good care of my baby, okay?" Vanessa nodded eagerly.

"You know I will, Connie. In fact, this one will be a bonus for me. I can't wait to take care of him."

Connie flipped a switch on the wall and smooth jazz drifted into the room. The two began to put on a show for me as their bodies automatically fell in sync with the music. Their legs and arms entwined like a braid. My head was propped up on the pillow, so I couldn't help but watch them through my droopy eyes. Connie turned around and touched her toes while Vanessa wound her pelvis into Connie's ass. Connie shot up like an arrow, and her hair fell down around her face.

Vanessa must have made Connie so horny with the way she caressed her ass that Connie couldn't take it anymore. It seemed like they had both forgotten I was in the room. Connie turned to Vanessa and plunged her tongue down her throat. Vanessa gripped Connie's supple ass and returned the kiss with equal passion.

Connie tore her lips away from Vanessa's and used them to form a trail from the base of Vanessa's neck to her belly button. Vanessa quivered as Connie approached her shaven pussy—it resembled a fuzzy peach that oozed of sweet juices. Connie sunk to her knees and examined Vanessa's clit as though she were trying to figure out exactly what she wanted to do to it.

Connie rubbed the hardened nub in a circular motion. Gently and slowly, then harder and faster. Vanessa's entire body began to quake and she moaned. Connie stole a glance upward, pleased that she was pleasing her. Vanessa groped the ringlets that Connie wore as a crown and brought Connie's head towards the destination she wanted met.

"I think she wants me to taste the pussy," Connie said, turning to me for the first time in a while to make sure I was paying attention. "Isn't it a pretty pussy, Chris?" I wasn't sure if I was capable of speaking. Connie kept her eyes on me and slipped her tongue out of the corner of her mouth. It must have followed the smell of sex that invaded the room, because Connie found her target without looking.

"That's right baby, eat that pussy," Vanessa purred. "Eat it all up. Lick that plate clean." I could see Connie's head bobbing up and down, just as it had when she went down on me. My dick lifted like an animal making sure it was okay to come out of its hiding place. Connie stopped for a moment and stood up. Vanessa was disappointed, but it wasn't long before Connie led her over to the bed. Vanessa lay down next to me and grinned, but neither one of them touched me. I knew it was a game of how riled up they could get me, and as much as I tried to keep Sylvia's face rooted in my mind, it was working.

This whole night offered two firsts for me—I had never seen two women fuck each other, in person anyway, and I had never had two people fuck right next to me.

"Don't worry, Chris," Connie said. "I'm just getting you up for what's about to go down."

Vanessa grinned over at me as Connie kneeled in between her legs. The music was suddenly drowned out by the slow lapping of Connie's tongue. Vanessa squirmed and her legs contracted as Connie's fervor increased. I could tell by the way Connie's head shook from side to side and she gripped the undersides of Vanessa's taut thighs. Vanessa sat up on her elbows to watch Connie perform her duty—she threw her head back in ecstasy and bit her full bottom lip. Connie inserted a finger inside Vanessa's sopping wet pussy which had now formed a dark spot on the bed.

That was enough to send Vanessa over the top and she arched her back so high that her head banged against the headboard. Connie reached upwards with her free hand and squeezed one of Vanessa's breasts that swung carelessly. She tugged the firm, opal nipple with her thumb and forefinger, and Vanessa howled.

Vanessa yanked Connie's head from the musky river that flowed from in between her legs, and just as quickly, she slammed Connie's face back into her pussy. Vanessa's hand snaked over my knee and up my thigh, and she groped my wooden dick as she came in Connie's mouth. Connie sat up and shot me a grin. The liquids that painted her face shone in the dim candlelight.

Connie paid Vanessa no mind now that she had brought her to a decadent completion. It was evident that she was ready to put all of her energy into me. But she didn't make a move. Connie shrank back from her voluptuous friend and tucked her knees under her chin. My temples began to throb and I was ready to go. I didn't care how hard my dick was or how drugged I was, I was still distraught over getting home to my wife. As my head began to clear, I became angry with the fact that Connie had brought another spider inside her web of deception.

As far as I knew, Vanessa hadn't had any wine, but her heavy eyelids said otherwise. I figured out why Connie hadn't attempted to jump my bones—she was waiting for Vanessa to do it. Vanessa had no intentions of disappointing her friend.

She swung a leg over my waist with no hesitation and tore at my belt buckle with a carnal desire I had never seen. She pulled my briefs and pants down just above my knee. Vanessa positioned herself over my dick froggystyle and lowered her body to meet her target. I didn't know this bitch, and she wanted me to bareback it? I jerked and thrashed about. Vanessa fell back angrily.

"What the fuck is wrong with you? What is wrong with this dude, Candy?" she asked, jabbing her thumb at me while looking back at Connie. "He scared of pussy or something?" Connie opened her mouth to speak but I jumped in first.

"You will not sit on this dick," I said, nodding towards my groin, "With that nasty cunt of yours!"

"What did you say?" Vanessa lunged at me, but Connie held an arm out in front of her. Vanessa grabbed Connie by the wrist, attempting to move her out of the way. "Fuck that! I aint lettin' no man talk to me like that, especially not no white boy!" Instead of responding, Connie's eyes narrowed and she snatched her arm away.

I was almost afraid for Vanessa's life with the look that Connie gave her.

"Look, if my man isn't comfortable with you riding him then that means I made a mistake," Connie said, "And you can leave." Even though I was pissed at Connie for having put me in this situation, I was grateful that she hadn't allowed this stranger to have her way with me. Vanessa leapt off the bed fully naked and placed her hands on her hips.

"Oh, I can leave? Well not without my goddamned money I won't!" she shrieked. Connie slowly stood from the bed, her face expressionless. She walked over to the nightstand and pulled a wad of cash from its drawer. Connie loosened the rubber band around the money and flung it at Vanessa. Vanessa was so enticed by the bills that floated down around her that she didn't see the heel of Connie's palm coming at her button nose. Connie knocked Vanessa on her ass with the speed of lightning.

"Didn't I tell you not to mention that? Didn't I, bitch?" Connie gave her a swift kick in the ribs and Vanessa clutched her side. "Get the hell outta here, trick." Vanessa gingerly touched her split bottom lip and swiped the back of her hand across her bleeding nose. Was this really going on in front of me?

First the two were going at it and now one of them was dripping blood all over the floor. Vanessa trembled with fury but it was obvious that she didn't dare test Connie. She simply gathered the bills from the floor without looking at either of us and dashed out of the room.

I had to get loose. Maybe this Vanessa girl could help me get out of this mess. Maybe she had something on Connie that I didn't. I would never know tonight because Connie was holding me captive. To top it all off, Connie had hired someone to screw me. I was over this bullshit. "Connie, I want you to untie me," I said through clenched teeth.

"Connie, I want you to untie me," she mimicked. "Don't worry about that bitch, Chris. Mama's gonna take care of you." I began screaming at her to untie me, throwing every curse word at her that I could think of. But Connie simply gave me a silly smile and climbed atop me. She planned to start where Vanessa had finished. She coaxed my throbbing dick towards what ached beneath her teddy, and I could feel myself entering her.

The sublime wetness was enough to take away all of the breath I used to yell at her. I suppose Connie knew that this would either shut me up or have me cursing at her for other reasons. She rode me with a smooth tranquility as I tried to remember to hate her. I could already feel her stickiness running down either of my thighs.

"Stop . . ." I murmured. "Please . . ." Connie ignored me and picked up her rhythm. My lower body twisted from side to side as her guttural moans ricocheted off the walls. I didn't know if I was trying to fight her off or drive myself deeper inside her warm and very welcoming pussy. Her lips and muscles embraced my dick and I knew I was going to cum. I felt one of her hands cupping and massaging my balls while she bit down on the pinky of her other hand. It was clear that she, too, was in a defiant battle with her rising orgasm, not wanting to succumb to the sweet agony.

I knew I was going to lose the fight first. Connie threw her head back and begged me to cum inside of her. Somewhere, in that tiny little portion of a man's brain that thinks when he's fucking, I knew that she wanted to trap me. She wanted me to get her pregnant.

"Don't . . . worry . . . can't get pregnant . . . I'm on the pill," she said breathlessly, as if jumping into my head. It wouldn't have mattered if she had told me anyway, because the eruption that was coming could not be stopped.

"Oh, shit!" I cried. Downstairs, I could hear the familiar ring tone that always let me know that my wife was calling me. Sylvia was probably trying to get in touch with me to see when I was coming home. Meanwhile, I was simply cumming.

Chapter 37

When I awoke the next morning, my hands were folded beneath my mussed hair. That meant that I was no longer a prisoner of Connie's boudoir and that I must have fallen asleep bound to the headboard. It felt as though someone had drilled a hole through both of my temples plus my forehead. I lifted my head, saw the pale lavender walls and burnt out candles, and instantly knew that I wasn't back at the hotel. I had a flight to catch and another wild night to try and forget. I turned my head to the right and caught sight of Connie's wild mane of curls.

She must have felt me stirring, because she turned to me. I tried to snap my eyes shut, but it was too late, and she knew I was awake. Besides, was I going to keep my eyes closed forever with the hopes that she would simply disappear? It didn't get easier for me to come to terms with the fact that Connie really would do anything to take me away from Sylvia. Why did I have to be the man that she latched on to? Better yet, why did I have to cheat for the first time with a crazy bitch? Things were only bound to get worse. I couldn't follow through with killing Connie—I still couldn't believe that had been an option for me—so I would have to get something else on her. Before I left Virginia, I was going to find that Vanessa girl. Something told me that she and Connie shared a deep past and an even deeper present.

First and foremost, I had to get back to my room. Connie had her leg thrown possessively over me and time was ticking. I needed to follow her around and get a general idea of who the real Connie was. If she was as big a liar as I thought she was, then she wasn't working behind some perfume booth. That wasn't paying her bills plus taking care of her son—she didn't strike me as the type to go from a stripper's wage to minimum wage overnight. I knew I was going to catch her doing something illegal. I could smell it just like the scent of her pussy all over me.

"What are you thinking about?" she asked. It was time to turn on the charm. With Connie, you had to use honey instead of vinegar. From now on, I had to watch my short fuse with her, because hers was a few inches shorter. But first, I had to get out of there.

"About us." She snuggled closer to me and smiled.

"Oh? What about us, sexy?" I playfully chucked her chin and forced a smile in return.

"I was thinking that I finally made a decision about us. Maybe you were right. Maybe this marriage thing isn't going to work." I was appalled at the excitement in her eyes. She threw her arms around my neck and I rolled my eyes when she couldn't see my face.

"You don't know how happy I am to here those words. And you know I don't give up easily . . . so all it took was bringing a little originality into the bedroom, huh?" Connie slid her hand underneath the sheet and began to run her hand up and down the shaft of my dick. I shyly swiped at her hand and said,

"I can't right now, baby. I have a flight to catch this morning and I have to get back home." Connie frowned slightly and then pouted.

“What about staying here a little longer with me?” I wrapped my arm around her shoulders and brought her head to mine.

“I plan on telling Sylvia when I get back.” She craned her head to look up at me and blinked twice.

“Are you serious, Chris? No bullshit?”

“No bullshit, baby. It’s time that you got your time with me. You were right . . . the bitch doesn’t support me like you do.” It put a bad taste in my mouth to talk about my wife like that, but I wanted Connie to believe me. I hoped she did, because she was nobody’s fool.

Connie began to probe the inside of my mouth with her tongue and it took a while before she pulled away from the deep kiss. I guessed that confirmed that she felt I was being genuine.

“You don’t know how happy I am to here that, Chris. I promise after we’re together I’ll help you take care of whatever’s needed at Balducci’s, and I’ll rub your back every night after you come home and maybe we’ll even plan a big, gorgeous wedding in the next year...”

As Connie went on and about our future plans, I hoped I hadn't gone too far.

If I didn't get any dirt on her, Connie would do everything in her power to make sure that I paid for the lie I had just told. "Well, can I take you to the airport?" she asked. Yet, another lie. I was going to do my investigating that day. My flight didn't depart until later on that night, but I knew if Connie found out, I wouldn't be able to keep her away from me until I left. I needed that precious time to follow her around and see what she was up to.

"Well, I was kind of hoping to catch up with Vince, so he's gonna be taking me. You know how it is when men get together."

"Of all people, you know I know!" she quipped. I wasn't in a laughing mood. I hoped she couldn't see my eagerness to leave etched in my tight smile. "I understand, baby. We'll talk about our plans after you get back to New York."

I bit back a sigh of relief and prayed that I wouldn't lengthen my list of mistakes in the future.

Chapter 38

I told the driver to park a few houses down from Connie's. I couldn't take the chance of her seeing me. As soon as I had arrived at the hotel, I took a brief shower, changed my clothes, and made a call to have someone pick me up and take me right back to her place.

The driver probably thought I was a stalker, a crazed ex-boyfriend, or both. I could tell by the way he glared at me over the reading glasses that slid down the bridge of his nose. Of course, he knew he shouldn't say a word as long as his meter ran. We sat there for a long time, but I knew that she hadn't left because her car was still in the driveway. Then again, there was always the possibility that someone had come to pick her up.

I was nodding off with the side of my face in my palm when the driver barked,

"There she goes."

"Huh?" I mumbled and stiffened when I saw her.

I could tell she was happy. Her pony-tail bounced from side to side and she had a brightly decorated gift bag in her hand. I wondered what was in the bag and where she was going with it. I was suspicious of anything that Connie did these days.

As she took off down the street, we followed suit. The driver made sure to stay at least three cars behind. It suggested to me that he had done this before. Connie drove about seven miles before turning into a well landscaped apartment complex. We drove into the lot parallel to where she had parked the Camaro.

"Is this your stop?" the driver asked. I ignored him and watched Connie march upstairs to the third floor. She rapped on someone's door, and once it opened, all I could make out were two, long brown legs and a pair of strappy sandals. "Man, are we doin' some illegal shit?" He asked too many questions.

"Look," I said, leaning forward. "We are not doing some illegal shit. The only thing you need to worry about is the amount of time we sit here. The longer your meter runs, the longer you get paid. Okay, buddy?"

The driver grunted and rolled his window down. A few seconds later, Connie came storming downstairs. I shivered because it reminded me of the first time I had seen her. This time she wasn't alone. Vanessa followed down behind her with tears streaming down her cheeks. They appeared to be arguing and Vanessa was clearly losing—Connie did most of the screaming. Vanessa placed an apologetic hand on Connie's shoulder and Connie responded by giving her a backhanded slap. The sound echoed throughout the complex.

"Oh, shit! I get it now—them bitches fightin' over you right?" the driver asked. I still didn't pay him any attention. I was too concerned with how Vanessa was going to retaliate, but she only clutched the side of her face and returned upstairs. Connie was right behind her with her fists clenched at her sides.

It was only a few seconds later that Connie came back holding the hand of a little boy at her side. I recognized Darren instantly. He resisted his mother, crying and tugging away from her. Eventually, Connie picked him up as they walked downstairs, put him in the backseat of her car, and buckled him in. She fumed as she ran around to the driver's side and started the ignition. The gravel popped underneath her squealing tires as she sped off. I waited a few minutes until I thought she was gone and the coast was clear. I told the driver to wait for me and I went to climb the stairs to Vanessa's apartment.

Chapter 39

I didn't know what Vanessa was going to do when I showed up at her door after the way I had spoken to her last night. I didn't know if she would shut it in my face. I didn't know if a man would answer the door and I didn't know if Connie was coming back. There were too many "didn't knows", but I was willing to take the risk.

She swung the door open, apparently thinking I was Connie. My first assumption had been right.

"Oh, hell no!" she shouted when she saw that it was me and promptly slammed the door in my face. I barely caught a glimpse of her red tear-streaked face.

"I'm not leaving until you listen to what I have to say!" I hollered and rested my forehead on her door.

"Get the fuck outta here before I call the police!"

"Go ahead! I'll tell them how we met." There was silence for a moment and then she unlocked the door.

"What the hell do you want?" She stood in the doorway wearing a loose fitting sundress. Her pixie face was devoid of any makeup except for the black crescents underneath her eyes from runny mascara.

"I want to know what Connie has on you." I could feel her preparing to close the door in my face again.

"Can't help you," she barked. I stuck my foot in the doorway to stop her.

"Or better yet, what you have on Connie."

"Still can't help you, now get the hell outta here." She tried to be brave, but her voice broke, and I knew she was scared of me.

"Fuck it," I said and pushed past her.

"Hey!" Balloons and "happy birthday" banners crowded her living room.

"Having a party like you did last night?"

"Shut your mouth," she hissed, glancing down her hallway. "I finally got my son to go to sleep, and I don't want your ignorant ass waking him up."

This calmed me down. I wasn't really pissed at her. I hadn't been pissed at her the night before either. She was only doing what Connie had paid her to. I was taking my frustrations with Connie out on Vanessa, and if I needed her help, this was not the way to get it. I decided to be honest with her.

"Look, I'm desperate. Connie wants to be with me, and if I give her one inkling that the feelings aren't mutual, she is going to do everything in her power to ruin my life. I'm sorry if I disrespected you but—" Vanessa held her hand up to stop me. She glanced back towards her son's bedroom again and gestured for me to follow her outside.

"You got a cigarette?" she asked.

"I don't smoke . . . often." A sad smile crept onto Vanessa's face.

"So, she got you too?" She leaned against the vinyl siding of her building and began to sob into her hands. I didn't know what she was talking about, so I let her cry it out. Vanessa shook with the last bit of tears she had in her then rubbed her eyes dry. "I must have looked like a damned fool last night. No offense, but I didn't want to fuck you, you know." I didn't respond, but I believed her. "Connie is a pro when it comes to ruining people's lives.

She'll find your weaknesses and . . . I hate that triflin' bitch."

"Well, I followed her over here and that's how I found you."

"I'm sorry to tell you, but finding something to pin on Connie is like having a black president—it ain't happened yet." I ran a hand through my hair, my impatience getting the best of me.

"What was she doing here today? And why did she slap the shit outta you?" I could tell that Vanessa was ashamed of what she was about to tell me, but she seemed to be relieved that someone else could empathize with her.

"Me and Connie met in high school, and, believe it or not, we used to be best friends."

"I sure can't tell."

"We had a lot in common then. My mom was dead, her mom was dead. She was raped by a family member . . . and so was I." My mouth twisted in disgust the same way it had when I found out about Gary. "My rapist just happened to be my father. He even taped it."

"That's some sick shit."

"I know. It made me sick. I would catch him watching it from time to time then I would run to the bathroom and throw up. I told Connie, and she said she would help me get rid of the tape . . . and Daddy, too."

"Kill him, you mean?" Vanessa nodded slowly.

"She said if she could ever pull it off with Gary, she could pull it off with Daddy, too. She *hated* Gary. She told me that she had put some stuff in his food once, and he had gotten sick. He didn't die and she was glad too, because she was sloppy. She said the next time, it wouldn't be that way." I felt nauseated when I thought of how many years she had to come up with the perfect murder. "Anyway, she said she had a good idea about how to get the tape. She was going to make it look like someone had broken into the house while I was at the mall and Daddy was out one Saturday. I told her I knew where he was hiding the tape and some money, and I told her that my dad always left the back door unlocked because we lived in a pretty good neighborhood. The day that she went in my house, Daddy was supposed to be fishing, but he came home sick. Connie brought another boy from the neighborhood to help her take some stuff.

I guess she slipped him the tape and he got away, but my dad grabbed her and told her she had to stay there until the police came."

"What happened then?"

"I came home, and she pleaded with me to tell my dad the truth about why she was really there. She said Gary would kill her if the police brought her home. She said she would go to the police with me and tell them what my dad had been doing to me. But I was too afraid, and I acted like I didn't know what she was talking about. I betrayed her."

I could tell Vanessa regretted that moment with everything in her.

"Connie was so hurt. And sooo angry. I will never forget how she looked at me that day. She turned to my dad, looked him dead in the eye, and told him she knew he had been fucking me, and if he pressed charges against her, the rest of the world would see that tape and know it, too. I had never seen my father piss his pants before, but I believe he did that day. When the police got there, he told them that he wasn't going to press charges, and they let her go. We were sixteen then, and Connie didn't speak to me again until a couple of weeks ago."

"So, I take it she never forgave you."

"I couldn't blame her for being angry with me then, but I never thought she'd take it this far."

"How far, Vanessa?"

"I had a job in the mall at a perfume booth. I would see Connie from time to time, and she would never speak to me until one day. She came right up to me and said she was tired of sleeping with some guy named Vince for extra money. She said she thought it would be best if I fucked a few rich white men for her and gave her seventy percent of what I made."

"And you just went along with it?"

"Hell no! I told her she must be out of her goddamned mind. She said she was perfectly sane and asked me if I had forgotten about the tape. I felt sick all over again, and by that time, my father had already passed with lung cancer—I thought my secret died with him. Connie said she would make sure that that tape got spread all over the internet and wouldn't it be a shame if my son ever found out I had fucked his grandfather. I couldn't let that happen, and I would die if my baby ever saw that tape let alone my friends and the rest of my family. So . . . I did it, and I recommended her to my boss so that she could have my job at Nordstroms." Vanessa stood, and I stood right along with her. Finally, I had someone in my corner.

"Extortion is a crime, Vanessa. If you and I go to the police, we can tell them what Connie has been doing to us." Hell, even if Connie did tell the police I had helped her kill Gary, they would have already established her as a liar, and I would convince them I had nothing to do with it. Vanessa could prove that Connie had been planning his murder all along. As for my wife, she would never have to find out about this mess in Virginia, and Connie would be tucked away in prison—

"There is no us. I don't even know your name."

"But we could help each other."

"No! I already have enough bullshit in my life. I don't need more drama. You obviously don't know how she is."

"No, I do know how she is, and I need your help to stop her."

"Look, I've already told you too much. It was crazy for me to even have you here this long. She's already pissed at me for missing an appointment." Vanessa glanced around to make sure no one was watching us. "Unfortunately, Darren and my son, Nick, became friends ever since Connie started stoppin' by with Darren to pick up her money. That's why he was here for Nick's birthday party. God forbid that bitch come back over here and catch me talking to you. Now, please leave." She headed back inside.

"But don't you want to be free to do as you please?" I pleaded with her. Vanessa paused at the door and turned back to look at me.

"I'm Connie's hoe now, and that's all I can be." Vanessa looked past me and gasped. "Leave me the fuck alone!" she shouted and turned around to run into her apartment. I looked over my shoulder, and my chest tightened. Connie had been watching us from her car and it was clear that she didn't believe Vanessa's sudden outburst. She knew I came over here to pump Vanessa for information and had probably received some. I expected her to race up the staircase kicking and screaming, but she simply gave me a blank stare and pulled out of the parking lot.

$$$$

I didn't hear anything from Connie for several months after that. Every day of those months I wondered if Connie had finally come to her senses and decided that this thing she had for me wasn't healthy. Fuck that "time heals all wounds" bullshit—sometimes, those wounds become infectious and spread. Something in me didn't feel immune to them. I wondered when I would get sick again.

$$$$

I believe it began one evening I came home late from Balducci's wrapped snugly in my coat, because the fall weather had set in. Connie had become a distant, but close, memory as each day passed, Gary's body had been found and buried with no leads, and Sylvia was starting to show. She had been a little distant when I returned home from the funeral, but I worked hard at being the kind and gentle husband who wouldn't hurt her sexually or otherwise. I came over to the leather couch where she lay. I kissed her forehead and rubbed her belly, grateful that I avoided the fate I could have been given.

It hurt to imagine myself behind bars as my wife and newborn visited me . . .

The fucked up thing was, I had a feeling that the hurricane I met with the full lips and hips was going to rain on my parade any day—the night sweats had returned. Bad sign. There were times I did want to call Connie, to soften her quiet anger. But my pride wouldn't let me do it, and I didn't want her thinking that the last face she gave me had gotten the best of me. It was the only other face I couldn't get out of my mind besides Gary's.

I had been dealing with his death pretty well until Connie forced me to go to his funeral and relive everything. After I returned home from that "visit," I couldn't stop waking up every morning in a pool of sweat from nightmares about the murder—sometimes, Sylvia's eyes would twinkle when she looked at me, and I saw the blood all over my hands. I didn't want to touch her with those hands when I first got back, because I thought she could see it too.

Once I saw that her expression wouldn't change, I would return her smile. Each day she greeted me that way, I began to forget. I sat down next to her. "You seem like you're in a good mood."

"That's because I have good news."

"You're mother is finally leaving?" Sylvia gave me a playful punch in the arm. Unfortunately, I wasn't joking. Although Elaine hadn't driven a wedge between me and Sylvia's happiness, she had been a constant thorn in my side for the last couple of friggin' months. She and Aldo couldn't hold a conversation for more than two minutes without him going off on her.

The longer she stayed here, the closer the two came to divorce. Already, she was thinking of changing the décor in our home that I secretly heard her tell Sylvia was subjected to my "lack of taste." Sylvia, meanwhile, was frequently caught in the middle of the little spats I had with Elaine. I didn't want to contribute to any of Sylvia's stress.

"Well, I have some news that might make her happy. Jerry called today."

"Oh, yeah? Did he find out anything about your grandfather?"

"He found out a lot of things about Mr. Dollar. Including where he lives."

"Are you serious? You know where he is?"

"Staten Island. Mariner's Harbor."

"So, what do you plan on doing with this information?"

"Well, I'm a little nervous about how my mom's going to take the news when she finds out that I've been snooping around, but my heart tells me that I'm making the right decision. Plus, I'm a little curious about meeting the man myself."

"In other words, you've already made your decision to pay him a visit?"

"I have an address. I was wondering if you could come with me tomorrow."

"Are you sure you're ready?"

"I want to do it before I get cold feet. Will you come?"

"Of course, I will. I have some business to take care of at the restaurant in the morning, but we can go afterwards." Sylvia embraced my lips with hers, and I felt the slow heat rising below my belt. Although the sex between us had been great the last couple of months, it had slowed down because of the pregnancy.

Suddenly, she pulled away and handed me a few envelopes from the end table. I tried not to show my frustration over her urgency to give me the mail and not what I really wanted.

"I forgot to tell you that you got this piece of mail today," she said. "It didn't have a return address."

My heart almost tore through my ribcage while I pretended to have the same curiosity as Sylvia. Opening the turquoise envelope with her green eyes boring into me was painstaking. I slowly pulled the note out and began to read the feminine scrawl. I didn't have finish it to know who sent it. I looked up at Sylvia and gave her a phony frown.

“They didn’t put a return address on it because somebody’s trying to sell me something.” I kissed Sylvia’s forehead. “I need to make a business call.” Sylvia’s eyes followed me into my study, and I closed the door behind me. Connie wrote the letter in vivid detail and described what she wanted to do to each part of my body. She had even included two pictures as further explanations. In each she was completely nude, fondling her breasts and other areas of her anatomy.

I ripped the photos into tiny shreds. If Sylvia’s curiosity had really gotten the best of her, she would have opened the letter and seen what was inside. I could see her now, clutching her pregnant stomach while sinking to the floor in anger and pain. I always knew that Connie didn’t give a damn if my wife found out. Maybe she even wanted that. She had promised me that this thing between her and I wasn’t over. I had to make up my mind since there were no other options—was I going to tell my wife, or was I going to let Connie do it?

Chapter 40

Sylvia and I headed down a quiet block towards the harbor. The colder air had crept up on us, but I knew she wasn't rubbing her hands together because of the weather. We were about to meet her grandfather for the first time. Neither one of us knew how he was going to react, considering we were coming by unannounced. She had asked me to turn around several times, but now, we were sitting in front of his house.

"Are you going to get out of the car?" she asked.

"Are you?" I said in return.

She laughed nervously and pulled her hat down over her ears. We approached the two-story brick home and a small black child with two long pigtails swung the door open. She watched us with big eyes, and I knew she wondered who these two white people were approaching the house. In fact, we both exchanged a look to determine if we had come to the right place. The little girl wasn't as intimidated as I thought.

"Are you looking for my Mom?" She had an adult's raspy voice. Sylvia smiled down at her.

"Who's your mom, sweetie?"

"Vernell Jackson. She's a case manager. Sometimes people got appointments with her."

"No, honey. That's not why we're here."

"Then who you looking for?" She stepped out under the awning with her hands on her hips.

"Nia! Get your behind in this house!" rumbled the loud bass behind the storm door. The little girl straightened up and went back to where she had come from. A tall brown man stepped out on the porch. His wrinkled face and long arms and legs resembled an oak tree. "Can I help you?"

"Um, yes . . ." Sylvia began. "I don't know if we have the right house though."

"Well, who are you looking for?"

"I'm looking for somebody named Jonathan Dollar."

"What do you want with him?" Sylvia and I looked at each other. So the elderly gentleman did know who he was.

"I think he's my grandfather." The man looked taken aback.

He squinted his eyes so tight at her that I thought he had closed them.

"What did you same your name was?"

"I didn't, sir. I just want to know if he used to live here. This was the address I was given."

"Well, I think you got the wrong place."

"But . . . you do know who he is?" The old man looked at us warily and walked back in the house. "Hey!" Sylvia huffed up the steps and rang the doorbell several times. No one responded to her helpless cries, and I pleaded with her to leave. "He knows who he is, Chris, I know he does!"

"Vee, let's just go. It's cold as hell, and I don't want him to call the police." The look on her face made me wish I could do something for her, but it was hopeless. This was the only lead that Jerry had given her. We turned to head down the walk when we heard the front door creak open again.

One look at Sylvia's wet eyes and I knew that I wasn't going to let the old bastard upset her again. The old man's face had softened, and the lines in his face seemed to smoothen out. "I'm sorry if I upset you, miss," he said. "I just don't know how I could have a white granddaughter."

Chapter 41

We sat inside of Jonathan's eat-in kitchen watching the street lamps give life to the fog outside. We sat with him for hours while Sylvia asked him questions about his whereabouts for the last fifty years. She had begun accusingly, wondering why he had never contacted Elaine. It turned out that Jonathan never even knew there was an Elaine.

He insisted that his relationship with Elaine's mother, Rosa, was a major taboo when they were young, and they had kept their relationship a secret. He knew that we were telling him the truth, because no one had known about them—a black man with an Italian woman was just making room for trouble then. One day, Rosa said she couldn't hide their affair anymore and called it off. Rosa had never told him about the pregnancy and to find that he had a mulatto daughter walking around seemed to be a lot to handle for him. Either Jonathan was a damned good actor, or he was sincere—he cried into his palms like a baby, and he and Sylvia clung to each other as though they had known about each other for years. I was happy for her, but I wondered how Elaine would take the news.

I knew she wasn't a racist, but I didn't know how she or her husband would accept this. Elaine had always led this fairy tale life with a phony past. But now that Jonathan had met his granddaughter, who seemed to immediately take to him, Elaine would have no choice but to admit that her father was alive and well and black.

Some people in her social class might not like it, but maybe this would knock her off that shitty high horse she rode around on. Besides, I thought about how happy it would make Sylvia to see Jonathan bouncing our child on his knee as he did Nia. Nia's mom, Vernell, was his oldest child. She lived with Jonathan to help him manage his diabetes.

"That's probably her right now," he said as we heard the familiar creaking of the front door. Vernell was a thin woman with darker skin than her father's, and her long hair was swept up into a bun.

Besides the fact that Vernell was a woman, she and Jonathan looked just alike. Vernell hummed a tune I didn't recognize, but the melody ended once she saw two strangers in her home. "Hey, Dad," she said, looking from me to Sylvia. "Are you going to introduce me to your guests?"

"Mommy," Nia cried, wrapping her gangly arms around one of Vernell's thighs, "Grandpa's got a daughter!"

"Yes," she said slowly. "The last time I checked I've been his daughter for more than forty years. So has your Aunt Marlene."

"I mean a *new* daughter."

"Nia, I think you should go to your room while the grown folks talk."

"Grandpa!" she whined. Jonathan shot the seven-year-old a warning glance. Nia didn't argue with him but stomped up the stairs.

"What is my child talking about?" Vernell asked.

"Vernell, I want you to meet Sylvia and—"

"Chris," I said.

She shook both of our hands and smiled as though she were about to be ambushed.

"Sit down, Vernell. I want to tell you who they are and why they're here."

"Okay." One could have made a motion picture out of the emotions that played across Vernell's face as he told her the story he had just told us. The genre went from drama to horror in a matter of minutes. Vernell focused her beady eyes on us like two bullets with either of our names on them.

She slammed her hands down on the kitchen table, shocking all of us with her immediate fervor.

"You can't possibly believe this shit, Dad!"

"Vernell, watch your mouth."

"Can't you see that they're lying?"

"I can assure you that we found the right man, Vernell," Sylvia said.

"Oh, you found the right man," she scoffed. "I just bet you did. How much money are you trying to get exactly?"

"What are you talking about?" I asked. "We didn't come here for money."

"Yeah, right. I know a hustle when I see one. Why my father, huh?"

"Vernell, I believe them. They know things they shouldn't," Jonathan said.

"Well, I'm sure they did their research."

"Sylvia is your blood."

"No, she's going to *see* blood if she doesn't get the hell outta here!"

The two women stared each other down, and I gripped my wife's forearm.

"Baby, I think we should leave," I said. Sylvia shrugged away from me and turned to Jonathan.

"You have my number if you want to talk further."

"Let me see you two out."

Vernell stood in the kitchen with her feet planted to the ground and her hands on her hips. Jonathan walked us to the car and gave Sylvia a hug.

"Don't pay Vernell any mind. She's always been very protective over me."

"That's understandable," she said. "But you have my cell number, and I'd like for you to call me so that you and my mother can meet."

"I would like that. I'll call you in about a week."

Chapter 42

Actually, it didn't take Jonathan a week to contact Sylvia. He called her two days later, and they talked like they were father and daughter ever since. Whenever Elaine came around, Sylvia would clam up and call him back later.

Meanwhile, Sylvia and I decided to throw a party at the restaurant to celebrate our wedding anniversary. We both wanted to do something where everyone could celebrate with us. We also thought it would be a great way for Matthew and Elaine to start talking again and for Elaine to finally meet her father. Sylvia put the word out to our closest friends and family about what we had planned. Everything was going right.

$$$$

I was on my way to meet with a young pro-football star by the name of Walter Davis. They called the twenty-year-old "Walt the Salt," because he could shake anyone on the field. He ate a meal at my place about two weeks prior to our meeting and began raving to my general manager about how good the dish was. Bobby had joked that if he liked the meal so much, perhaps he should endorse the restaurant. Walt said that didn't sound like such a bad idea and that maybe he and I should talk. I was reminded again of why I loved Bobby so much.

My hostess told me that Walt was seated with his agent in the v.i.p. area the employees called "the black room." The walls, the tabletops, and the seats were laden with black European silk. Walt stood as I approached, and I had to look up at least a foot above my own head. He was as broad as the room itself and his tone was golden. He was a hot commodity on the sports scene, and the women loved him. Balducci's would do well having him on its team.

"Mr. Balducci?"

"Call me Chris," I said, extending my hand.

"This is my agent, Harvey Weintraub." The tiny Jewish man nodded his head at me and adjusted his glasses. I took it from that small gesture that Walt was mature enough to make many of his own decisions and that his agent would sit on the sidelines. Walt and I talked for about an hour, and I really did like the kid. He seemed to have his head on straight, and we even talked about doing a commercial. By the time we finished meeting, and of course eating, Walt and I had planned to get together again later on during the week. I walked him outside and he noticed my car.

"That's a tight whip!" he exclaimed. I may not have been familiar with all youthful slang, but I knew that meant that he liked my car.

"Thanks. Though I'm sure you have something even better. You want to take it for a drive?"

"Yeah, man. Why not?" Mr. Weintraub told Walt he would speak with him later, and Walt climbed into the driver's seat of my car. Ordinarily, I didn't let anyone drive my car but me. However, I wanted everything to go smoothly with the endorsement, so I allowed it. We weren't driving around for long when I noticed a putrid smell coming from somewhere inside my car. I gave Walt an uneasy glance out of my peripheral vision, and I wondered if he had caught a whiff of it too.

Although it was freezing outside, Walt rolled down his window, and I figured that he had smelled the stench. What the hell was that? It was beginning to make me physically ill.

"You smell that?" he asked, wrinkling up his nose.

"Yeah. I'm trying to figure out where it's coming from."

"It's beginning to make me feel a little sick."

"Me, too. Let's just turn around and go back to the restaurant so that I can figure out where it's coming from." Walt made a u-turn and headed back towards Balducci's. By the time we pulled into the parking lot, the odor had grown even worse. I went to grab some napkins from my glove compartment to cover my nose. When I opened it, a flurry of white and red fell to my feet.

"What the hell is that?" Walt said. I was so disgusted, I almost fell out of my car door. Walt leapt out of his side of the car once he realized what they were. "What kind of sick shit is that, man?"

"Wait a minute, I don't know how this shit got in here—"

“Fuck that! I’m out.”

“Walt! Wait a minute.” He ignored me as he climbed into his 2007 Range Rover and squealed out of the parking lot. I had just lost an important customer and an endorsement. All because that bitch had put a slew of used tampons in my glove compartment.

Chapter 43

I sanitized my car before returning home, and never before did I want to grind someone's face into the ground as I did Connie's. I knew she had done this. She was the only person who would have done something like that, and I had no idea how she broke into my car. It infuriated me that she was somewhere hanging around and had probably watched and laughed at me as I had scrubbed away. I had to put an end to this, to find my footing as my feet scraped the floor like a puppet at Connie's bidding.

A slow anxiety stole into my heart, because her antics were becoming more extreme. Already, I had lost a chance at making unspeakable money. She ruined everything with one despicable act.

I could hear Walt relaying the story to his very famous and very rich football buddies. I might even lose business instead of bring it in like I had originally planned. As a last resort, I called Vince on my cell phone as I headed home. Maybe he would know what to do about

Connie. Why hadn't I thought of my cousin before?

"Hey, cousin? What's going on?" Vince was his usual jovial self. He sounded like the exact opposite of me. I started from the beginning all the way to the incident with the feminine products, finally admitting to Vince that I hadn't called it off with Connie when I said I had.

"Not for nothing, I warned you, Chris."

"Look, I know it was stupid. At the time, I felt bad for her. We both needed each other for different reasons. I gave into temptation, and you know the rest. I came to my senses, she didn't."

"Well, what do you want me to do?"

"I want you to help me, goddammit! The bitch is crazy. Do you know how much blood I cleaned out of my car today?"

"I didn't know she was that off. She never went that far with me. Then again, Connie and I had very specific guidelines in our relationship and feelings were never an issue."

"I know. I am so fucking stupid! I can't believe I was so weak. I should have focused on my marriage and not a piece of ass."

"It happens to everybody, Chris. You just didn't wake up in time."

"You said Connie never went that far with you. Just how far did she go?"

"You know, calling me all hours of the night. Showing up at my place unannounced, shit like that. But I think that was mostly about the money. She knew about the other broads, and she wasn't trying to play second fiddle to any of them—they might cut into her funds. Of course with you, it was different. You treated Connie like a lady." Vince snickered and instantly quieted when he saw that I wasn't joining in. "Why don't you offer her something?"

"What are you talking about? Money?" I didn't want to give her a damned dime. "That's not what she wants from me."

"Maybe not. Maybe she does want you, because she thinks she's in love with you. But there is one guy that she loves more—her son. Think of what a nice lump sum of money could do for their lives. I know Connie certainly will if you pitch it to her that way."

"She could ask for a shitload of money, you do know that?"

"How much is your marriage worth?" Vince had a point there. I had fucked up, and now it was time to pay the piper. However much Connie asked for, I would just have to eat it. Sylvia would not be the one to pay for what I did to her. Connie did love Darren more than me, of that much I was sure. I told Vince I would think about what he had said as I pulled into my driveway.

It started to rain and the sky began to unleash large pellets of hail. I forgot the weatherman had called for a thunderstorm that evening. I pulled out the remote to open my garage door when I noticed a flash of lavender moving at a runner's pace towards me. Elaine was sprinting down the sidewalk through the rain, and although it was as thick as a sheet, I could still see the maniacal look in her eyes. Her jogging suit clung possessively to her body, but she didn't seem to mind or notice how it was pouring outside.

"What the hell?" I mouthed. I had never seen Elaine have a manic episode before though Sylvia had informed me that she hadn't been taking her medicine lately. I didn't have to see an episode to recognize one. This was not the posh, sensible Elaine I knew who wouldn't dare let her hair look like that in public. I jumped out of the car against my better judgment.

She and I might not have liked each other, but I knew Sylvia would have a fit if she knew her mother was outside like this. The rain immediately plastered my hair to my head, and I called out to Elaine. Instead of responding, Elaine ran right into me, almost knocking me over. I was irritated, but that didn't stop her from laughing wildly. She swiped the bangs out of her face.

"This feels great, Chris! You should try it."

"What the hell are you doing? Are you trying to catch pneumonia?"

"Oh, please. You only live once right? I love the rain on my face! It makes me feel alive."

"Elaine, it's starting to thunder and lightning very badly out here. It's not safe. I think you should come inside."

"Aren't you tired of living by boring rules? Playing it safe all the time? Do something everybody else isn't doing goddammit. I'm tired of having a stick stuck up my fucking ass all the time." I was worried now. The night that Elaine and I had talked in my study, she had been going through one of her low points. Now, she was hyper and irrational, and I didn't know how to handle it. I just wanted to get her in the house and get her to shutup. Although the rain drowned out most of her ranting, she was still shouting very loudly, and I waited for the neighbors to come out.

"Elaine, I promise the next time it comes down like this, I'll come running with you. But today, I'm tired. Why don't you use some of that energy to help Sylvia plan a baby shower or something?"

She seemed to go for this and nodded her head quickly. I opened up the garage and drove my car inside. Sometimes, I would leave it in the driveway since it was less of a hassle in the morning, but never again after what Connie had done. I waited for Elaine to follow behind me, and then I closed the garage door. I stepped out of the car and attempted to squeeze some of the rain from my soaking sweater. I rested my back against the driver-side door and took off my water-filled shoes one by one.

Elaine followed suit and gave me a funny look. "Remember what I said earlier?" she asked.

"What?"

"That you only live once." Elaine took a step towards me while she unzipped the top half of her jogging suit. I stood there in wide-eyed shock, unsure of what she was going to do next. Elaine revealed that she wasn't wearing a bra. Her nipples stood at attention as though they wanted to be sucked. I tore my eyes away from her and looked at my bare feet.

"What the hell are you doing?"

"Don't fight it, Chris." She planted her lips on mine. I struggled to get away from her, but one of her arms was crooked tightly around the back of my neck.

"Fight what?" I tried to ask before she stuck her tongue back in my mouth. She groped the lump in between my legs that rose against my will. Elaine's hands and wrists were as slippery as a fish out of water and it was hard for me to pull them away. She unzipped my pants, and I swore that Sylvia could hear it. Elaine pulled my swollen dick free of its cotton prison and dropped to her knees. She swallowed me whole, and my legs convulsed. I grabbed a handful of Elaine's hair as she coated the length of me with her warm mouth. I couldn't believe that my mother-in-law was going down on me in my garage. My head spun as the blood drained down to where my dick disappeared and reappeared. I remembered the last time I felt that way. The guilt and the pleasure all at the same time. Connie held my livelihood in her grasp, because I had allowed her to. It would destroy Sylvia if she ever found out I betrayed her with another woman, but it would kill her if she found out that one of those women was her own mother.

This time when my leg convulsed, it was because I jerked away from Elaine. She lost her grip and fell back on her elbows, letting out a yelp. Elaine winced in pain and looked away sheepishly. I put away my erection, and she zipped up her top. The door from the kitchen to the garage swung open, and Sylvia frowned down at her mother.

Chapter 44

"**Mom? Chris? What's** going on?" Elaine's faced turned a reddish color, and the disheveled hair around her face gave her the appearance of a lion. Elaine gestured towards the wall unit behind her where I kept most of my tools.

"I was trying to reach something on the top shelf, and I fell." I turned and placed my hands on the roof of the car to hide my pending erection. I gave Sylvia a tight smile and secretly slid my shoes back on—she would have certainly wondered when I had the time to remove them.

"Hey, babe. I must have scared your mom when I pulled into the garage." Sylvia ignored me and turned on her mother.

"What were you looking for, Mom?" Elaine's eyes dashed about and I knew she had no idea what was on that shelf.

"Umm . . . light bulbs, sweetheart." Sylvia extended a hand to help Elaine to her feet.

"We keep them in the kitchen, Mom." Her tone was highly irate, and I wondered if she had heard anything before she walked in. “I was worried about you. What in the world made you decide to run out of this house in the pouring rain?” Elaine focused on wringing out her jogging suit.

“I didn’t realize—”

“Oh, you realized. It was raining before you left this house.” Elaine raised her haughty chin, and this time, she stared squarely at her daughter.

“I don’t have to explain myself to you, young lady. Besides, I have always exercised to keep all of this up. Imagine what my friends at the club would say if I let myself go. A little rain isn’t going to stop me.”

“Mom—”

“I’m going to take a nap. My nerves are already bad after nearly being mowed down.” Elaine shot me a look before she walked inside the house, but I wasn’t fooled. Her green eyes were darker, begging me not to tell Sylvia what she had just finished doing. Once I thought my dick had calmed, I turned to my wife and held her in my arms for a long time.

"She hasn't been taking her meds," she said into my neck. Today had been a crazy one. First the embarrassing episode with Walt, and now, with Elaine. "But I did speak to Jonathan today, and he wants to come to our anniversary party. He thinks it's time that he meets his daughter."

"I think it'll do your mother some good." Sickness or not, I was going to get Elaine focused on something else besides me. I had no idea what came over her this afternoon, and I didn't know if she would try to pull that stunt again, but I wasn't having it. She had committed the ultimate betrayal, and Sylvia just might kill her if she ever found out. My wife could be as sweet as pie, but when she was angry, she had a mean streak just like her father's that stretched as long as the New Jersey turnpike. I hoped that Elaine's meeting with her father would go well. As soon as she was happy, she could put all of that positive energy back into her marriage and put that mouth of hers on her husband where it belonged.

Chapter 45

Sylvia was on cloud nine. I had sent her five dozen long-stemmed red roses. Our anniversary dinner was that night, and Jonathan had called to ask for directions to the restaurant. All of our closest friends were coming, and Vince was supposed to be flying into town. Sylvia wasn't particularly happy about my cousin showing up. The two of them never really did have much to say to each other, because she thought Vince was a womanizer.

Although that was a fact, I always reassured Sylvia that none of Vince's bad habits had rubbed off on me. That much was still true since my cheating was never his fault. In fact, I had kept my affair hidden from him for quite a while too. The incident with Connie and my car had happened about two weeks ago, and I tried to call her cell phone ever since. Surprisingly, she never answered, and then, I really began to wonder what she was up to. There was no way she had gone from confessing her love, to vandalizing my car, to ignoring me altogether. I had actually planned to smooth things over with her by the time we had the party so that I could celebrate comfortably and get on with my life. But Connie was still one extra headache besides the one I was getting from planning the big event.

Carla had done most of the work. It appeared that she was an expert at decorating as well as cooking. White lights were strung about the entire restaurant. She had covered every table with white linen cloths—a vase filled with white lilies sat atop each.

Everyone was asked to wear white that night. Pictures of me and Sylvia hung on the walls, and a soft shroud of white rose petals covered the floor. Even the fish in the pond had been replaced by floating ivory candles that gave off an intoxicating scent of vanilla. An ice sculpture of a couple holding on to each other would be brought in later. A jazz band would entertain since Sylvia and I had enjoyed our first date at the popular Village Vanguard.

I wanted everything to be perfect and to make everything right between us for good.

$$$$

I went to pick up my white linen suit I had ordered and headed home to change. Sylvia wasn't there. She had mentioned something about buying a dress at the last minute with her mother. That was fine by me, because the less time I had to spend around Elaine, the better. Sylvia should have been stepping through the door any minute, or she was going to be late.

A loud sound like a glass smashing against the floor rang out from my master bedroom. I crept to our walk-in closet and pulled down my bat from the top shelf. Even though I didn't carry it in my car anymore, that didn't mean I couldn't keep it in my house. The bathroom door was slightly ajar, and I held the bat in both of my hands with a steady grip. I kicked the door in and let out a battle cry. Sylvia was kneeling on the floor, but she jolted and froze as she saw me coming towards her with the bat. Immediately, I stopped, and we both looked at each other before we started laughing. "What the hell were you doing?" she asked.

"I didn't know you were home. I didn't even see your car. Anyone could have been in here."

"You have been mighty jumpy these days. I just dropped my mirror, that's all."

I placed the bat on the floor and helped her pick up the broken glass.

"Where's your, mom?"

"She took my car to her house."

"Is your father there?"

"Yep. I managed to get them to start talking again. I told them I wanted them to arrive together to our party. He didn't promise anything else, but he said they would do that."

"Well, that's a start. Hey, you know what they say about breaking mirrors."

"Seven years of bad luck." I lifted Sylvia over the sink and tucked myself in between her legs. "We're going to be late, Chris," she said.

I started a trail of kisses from her inner knee to her inner thigh. Sylvia threw her head back with a low moan as my mouth searched a little higher. I slid the moist satin aside and plunged my tongue inside of her. I could feel her pulsing against my lips, and her clit began to do a little dance with my mouth. I looked up at her. “I’m not superstitious,” I said.

Chapter 46

I rented an ivory 2007 Rolls Royce Phantom for the night. When we pulled up to our event, a white carpet adorned with a string of lights and rose petals waited for our footsteps. The soft lull of smooth jazz beckoned us into Balducci's—I would have to start making the place look like this more often. Cheers and applause greeted us, and I felt like someone famous. I didn't know how Sylvia managed in her heels, but she pulled it off effortlessly. She must have been glowing brighter than the lights surrounding us, because everyone was smiling at her.

I knew that Vince would be disappointed about missing his flight once I told him all of my wife's sexy cousins had shown up. Even Aldo, whose face was usually tighter than a pussy, seemed happy with seeing his only child pleased and very pregnant. Of course, it was probably an act he put on for his colleagues. I glanced around the room and nodded my hello to everyone who had decided to attend when I saw a face in the corner that wasn't smiling. My confident steps and grin faltered as I stared back at her. She was the only person in the room who was out of place, defiantly wearing the black dress she had donned when we went out dancing months ago. Connie's hair was gathered back into a twist and to an outsider, she would have appeared to be a demure socialite—her looks had had me fooled. But I knew the truth.

She stood in that corner seething, and her anger fed off of my wife's joy. I regained my composure, realizing that the cameras were still flashing, and everyone was still watching us. We sat at our designated table with Sylvia's parents. I wished mine could have been there.

"Chris, it's been a long time," Aldo said and shook my hand.

Although he was a snob himself, he didn't totally overlook the fact that I was a hard worker, and he respected my ethic, unlike his wife. Elaine barely mumbled two words to me, but I was hardly concerned with her guilty conscience at this point. I wanted Connie to make a move and be done with it, because frankly, the waiting was killing me. Aldo had invited a couple of his boardroom buddies, and I tried to engage myself in their Wall Street bullshit. I didn't want it to appear as though I was distracted and that my eyes wouldn't stop roaming to a particular area in the room. What the hell was she doing here? She had some nerve, popping up like that on me and Sylvia's night.

Of course, after what she had done to my car, I guess I should have expected something this brazen. The next time I had an after-hours affair like this, everyone would have to show their invitations at the door. Our guests commented on how delicious the food was, and occasionally, I glanced over at Connie who sat eating with a group of some of my closest friends.

"Did you hear what I said?" Sylvia asked me. I looked at her, dumbfounded. "They want us to start off the dancing." Sylvia and I stood and went to the middle of the floor that was cleared specifically for everybody who wanted to get drunk and have a good time. We held each other and danced to a melody by Mariah Carey that we played at our wedding. Everyone else began to gather around us and dance with their significant others. Even Matthew and Elaine swayed to the music, and she clung to him as though she didn't want to let go—she was being on her best behavior. I didn't know if she was still in love with her husband, but I did know that she had grown to love being rich. Elaine had never worked a day in her life since being with Aldo, and she could never get used to it.

I would try to forget what she had done to me and write it off as her illness. But if she ever disrespected me again, I would remind her of what she did. If she threatened to tell Sylvia I had come on to her to break up my marriage, it would be my word against a woman who had gone jogging during a hailstorm. Sylvia winced and clutched her stomach.

"You alright, baby?" I asked.

"Yeah. Probably just a little indigestion. I think I need to sit down for a minute."

"Then you won't mind me cutting in?" Sylvia looked past me and at the owner of that voice.

"I'm sorry, do I know you?" she asked. Connie giggled and shook Sylvia's hand.

"Constance. Chris and I went to high school together." I gawked at her.

"Sylvia Balducci. I can't believe we've never met. It's nice to meet you."

"You should have seen your husband in high school. He was the class clown."

"Really? I guess he's a serious old man now."

"Oh yeah, Chris was always playing games."

"Well, you'll have to share some stories with me. Listen, I don't mean to be rude, but I really do have to sit down now. You and Chris can play catch up." Silently, I begged her to stay, but Sylvia walked away, because she didn't know that she should be worried. Connie blinked her eyelashes at me with mock innocence.

"Well?"

"Well, what?" I spat out.

"Are you just going to let me stand here?" I pulled Connie to me with my left arm and clasped her left hand with my right.

"I should knock you out," I whispered.

"Now, Chris. That's no way to speak to a lady."

"Show me a lady, and I'll show you how to address one—what are you doing here, Connie?"

"Even though you tried to betray me with that little bitch Vanessa, I still came to get what's mine. I love you too much to let you go that easily."

"Leave her out of it, Connie. And I was never yours." Connie's fingers clung to the back of my neck like a tarantula—each time her red talons grazed my skin, I felt like she was injecting her venom. I noticed that several people were watching us intently. I wondered if it was obvious that Connie was throwing herself at me.

I sneaked a peek at my wife who sipped on a glass of ginger ale. Her eyes met mine, and she smiled, completely oblivious to the way Connie had become my second skin. Then again, Sylvia had never worried about other women catching my eye. The only thing she had ever felt the need to compete with was my business, and we barely argued about that anymore since I had become more focused on my family. I felt like shit, because Sylvia was so trusting of me. Connie let out a soft snort in my ear.

“The perfect little family. How proud you must be.” I pulled Connie tighter, and not because I wanted her closer to me, but because I wanted to cut off her circulation.

“Perhaps if you were more concerned with your own, you might have the same.” That struck a nerve. She went as stiff as a board.

“Are you implying that I don’t know how to take care of my child?” I was glad that I had wiped that smug smile off of her face but I didn’t want her doing anything irrational, so I softened my approach.

“Connie, I think it’s time we talk one on one. Meet me in my office in about ten minutes. It’s to the left of the ladies’ room.” Connie dropped the attitude and seemed content with this. She released me, gave Sylvia a little wave, and went back to the table she had chosen amongst strangers.

Her dress swept through the sea of white like a dark cloud and every male eye in the room was on that captivating woman. I knew better. Connie’s searing, coffee eyes scalded me from across the room as she counted down each minute I kissed my wife, rubbed her tummy, or shared a private joke with her. It truly pissed me off that she was making what was supposed to be a memorable moment a very uncomfortable one. I went over to my table and threw back some wine. I looked at my wife questioningly when I realized she had been trying to ask me something again.

"Chris, are you here with me?"

"I'm sorry, baby, what did you say?"

"I was talking about your friend, Connie. Is she single?" The wine stopped about halfway down my throat, and I fought back a strangled cough.

"Why do you ask?"

"Well, my old co-worker, Freddy, expressed some interest in her. After all, she is a very beautiful woman, and she looks so young." I knew Freddy, and I liked the guy. That's why I had no intention of playing matchmaker when it came to Connie.

"I don't think that would be such a good idea."

"Why not? He isn't her type?" Freddy resembled a young Denzel in Richochet and was now a senior partner at his own firm. He was definitely Connie's type. I would have to come up with some other bullshit to feed my wife.

"Well, she's just getting over a nasty divorce, and she's from out of town. I doubt a long-distance relationship is what she needs right now."

"Well, I told Freddy you'd ask her if she's interested." I sought out Connie's table and saw that she had disappeared. If I was going to negotiate some kind of financial plan to get rid of her, the time was now. I excused myself, complaining of a sudden urge to jump on the toilet, and headed towards the bathrooms.

Chapter 47

Even if I had been walking with a blindfold on, I could have followed Connie's scent all the way to my office. When I walked through the door, I had already planned what I was going to say to Connie in regards to the money. I knew that Connie had other plans once I saw the dress and the Victoria Secret's panty and bra set flung across my leather chair. She had chosen to drape her body across my desk wearing nothing but a pair of Guccis.

Although my dick sometimes had a mind of its own, there was no underlying attraction to Connie beyond that. Connie's true character was just as naked to me as the rest of her. I would think with the head on top of my shoulders. At that moment, there were no drugs, and there was no bullshit involved. The lamp shone over her skin like the sun against the tawny coat of a cheetah. I didn't wait for her to pounce.

"I think you need to put some clothes on, Connie."

"No one knows we're together, Chris. I know we can't be long. But I can work with time constraints." She swung her legs over the front of the desk and spread them like the wings of an eagle, exposing a moist, pink cleft. I held her steady gaze.

"That's not what I want from you, Connie." She replaced her hungry look with a gentleness I thought I had seen in her before, and she quietly put her clothes back on. She came to me with her arms outstretched and buried her face and curly tendrils in my neck.

"I knew you still cared. I knew if you saw me again you would change your mind. It never was just about the sex with me, was it?" I hesitated and placed my hands on the small of her back. I would have to handle this delicately. I decided not to do it here. If Connie chose to blow up, I didn't want it to be at my anniversary party for all to see.

"There's something I want to give you, Connie, but not here." She pulled a post-it off my desk and wrote something on it. Connie pressed her ruby lips against the paper and handed it to me.

"This is where I'm staying. I'm checking out tomorrow, and I know you can't get out of here right now, but come later on tonight." I remembered the last time I met Connie at a hotel, and even though I didn't want to go, I knew I had to settle things with her sooner or later. She was a problem I wanted solved immediately. A problem that could cause too many others.

$$$$

Connie and I had only been in my office for five minutes, but it felt like five hours. A lot can happen in five minutes. Elaine's hand was held high in mid-toast when I went back out there. She should have been giving the crowd a fake smile as she congratulated her daughter on her nine-year marriage, but she was as frozen as everyone else, and I turned to see what they were all looking at.

A man stood rooted in the middle of the floor like a regal oak tree. It was Jonathan Dollar. His eyes streamed with tears upon recognizing his daughter, and he buried his face in his hands. I stood back and watched as he approached our table, crying out Elaine's name. "I didn't know, baby," he said. "I am so sorry . . . you are more beautiful than I ever imagined. Just like your mother was." Aldo and his friends exchanged a few embarrassed looks. Elaine's eyes darted around nervously, trying to figure out what this man was talking about and why he had stolen her moment.

"I'm sorry, sir, but who are you?" she stuttered. Jonathan wrinkled his brow and took the glass from Elaine's hand so that he could take both of her hands into his own. Once Sylvia saw the puzzled look on her mother's face, she stood to explain but Jonathan beat her to it.

"It's me, baby, your father." Aldo jumped from his chair almost knocking it over.

"What the hell is this? Who are you?" His associates exchanged whispers and looks, some surprised and others disapproving.

I believe Jonathan's tear-stained face was the last one Elaine saw before she hit the floor.

Chapter 48

We stayed at the hospital all night. Elaine had gained consciousness, but she wasn't speaking. A nurse propped Elaine's head up against the starched, white pillows while Elaine stared at the wall. I had never seen her look so bad, though the doctor said she was probably just in shock. The nasty bump on her forehead only made her appearance worse. Sylvia sat at Elaine's bedside while Jonathan and I talked quietly in the hallway.

Aldo refused to come to the hospital while "that man" was there. He couldn't get over the fact that Jonathan was black. I guess the bigots are revealed when color is staring right in the faces of their families and colleagues. My father-in-law had taken me and my wife to the hospital in his limo. He sat in stony silence the entire time. After Sylvia had told him Jonathan was telling the truth and that it was our bright idea to surprise Elaine at the party, he didn't have too much to say to either one of us—he left the hospital shortly after.

"I think I should try and talk to her. I didn't mean to scare her by getting so emotional. I thought she knew I was coming."

"Well, I could see why you got that way after seeing your oldest daughter for the first time. It's been over fifty years of not knowing she was alive."

"I don't know what to do. I don't want her to get even more upset."

"The worst she can do is ask you to leave her alone. And it must not be that bad if they're only keeping her overnight." Jonathan mulled this over as he clasped his chestnut hands together. He peeked into the room, and Sylvia gave him a sad smile. Something seemed to flicker in Elaine's eyes, and they turned an emerald color I had never seen. She turned to Jonathan and stared at him for a long time. Sylvia decided to leave the father and daughter alone.

$$$$

"My father is a fucking asshole," Sylvia said after we arrived home that night.

"I feel like calling him and telling him so."

"Sylvia, chill out. You don't need to get pissed off and stressed out while you're carrying the baby."

"I'm thinking about the baby, but I'm thinking about my mother too." A brief vision crossed my mind of Elaine not thinking of Sylvia while she had my dick in her mouth. "He didn't even have the decency to bring his ass inside the hospital after she almost split her head open."

"Your father has always been about image—it's nothing new, Sylvia."

"Well, he needs to be reminded from time to time that the world doesn't revolve around him." She hit the speed dial button for her father's house and put on the speakerphone. He picked up after the third ring as Sylvia pulled her maternity gown over her head.

"Yes?" he snapped.

"Why the hell aren't you over there with your wife?"

"How dare you call my house using that tone of voice?"

"It's one you should be familiar with using, Dad."

"Don't be a wise ass. And I don't have to explain a damned thing to you after what you and your husband pulled tonight." Suddenly, he had forgotten my name when I did something he didn't like.

"What did we do that was so bad, huh? Reunite my mother with her birth father?"

"I have a reputation to uphold. A reputation that I kept all these years even though I was a young fool that married my housekeeper's daughter. Now, that secret is probably going to come out since you introduced your mother to that man from the projects."

"That man has a name. It's Jonathan Dollar, and he lives in a respectable neighborhood just like you. He also happens to be my grandfather and will be my child's great-grandfather."

"I'm not having anything to do with him, and neither will your mother, as long as she's my wife. After all these years of having no ties to her whatsoever, he can't be more than a nigger that's after your mother's money, which happens to be *my* money."

"You disgust me."

"For someone who dropped out of law school and is now nothing more than a housewife, I could say the same to you." Sylvia's bottom lip trembled, and I could tell she was going to lose this argument much like the others she had had with her father. This time, I witnessed his cruelty, and I stalked across the room to hang up the phone. I stood there holding her quivering body, whispering that nothing he had said was true. It would be less than twenty-four hours later that I would encounter another angry female, and her fury wouldn't be as quiet as Sylvia's had become.

Chapter 49

It was barely dawn as I crossed the parking lot to my restaurant, and the brittle New York air made my nose crack. I wanted to get started on the mess my employees couldn't get to the night before due to the drama that had unfolded. My brisk walk turned into a sprint when the Camaro careened around the corner right at me. Connie's car jumped the curb in front of Balducci's and came to an abrupt halt underneath its awning. I stumbled and fell to the ground with Connie's fender hovering over my feet. Connie jumped out of the car and left it running.

"Where were you?"

"Connie? What the hell is wrong with you?" Once I stood up, Connie came at me with flailing arms. She grazed me under one eye with an acrylic nail, and I gripped both her wrists when she clawed at me again.

"Calm the fuck down!"

"Fuck you, Chris!" I glanced around to make sure no one was watching and spun Connie around so that her back was to me. I dragged Connie over to her car, turned the ignition off and kicked the door shut after taking out the keys. Connie screamed like a banshee as I unlocked the door to my restaurant and shoved her inside. Connie toppled onto the floor and her denim mini-skirt rose up around all that brown thunder. Carla stepped from the kitchen into the dining area and watched us from across the room.

My face flushed, because I had no idea that anyone was coming in that early besides me. But Carla was so dependable, I guess I should have known that her husband would drop her off to help me that morning. Connie spun around and glared at her even though she was the one with the exposed thong.

"Is everything okay, Chris?" Carla stammered.

"Does it look like it?" Connie screamed. I ground my teeth so hard that I thought I would break my jaw.

"Could you excuse us?" I asked. Carla was dumbfounded, caught in the middle of an obvious affair. She backed out of the room and returned to her duties in the kitchen.

Connie's eyes were boiling now.

"You were supposed to meet me last night."

"In case you hadn't noticed, I was throwing an anniversary party. I couldn't just up and leave."

"Did your fat ass wife sit on top of you or something?"

"You have one more time to disrespect her."

"She's no good for you Chris—I am."

"Look at what you're doing, Connie. You just got a new job, and you're here. You have classes to finish, and you're here. I need a woman who has her priorities straight, not one that acts like a fucking maniac."

"Well, I guess I'm crazy in love. I came all the way up here to see you Chris, because I'm in love with you, and I know what you really need is a woman who will support your ambitions, not dig a grave for them."

"Connie, we got together at a time where we were both weak and needed to lean on each other. But that time has passed. The love I have for my wife *never* will."

"So, you used me is what you're saying."

"We used each other."

"You know, you sound like your bullshittin' cousin right now."

"Vince never promised you anything. You were just after him for his money anyway."

"Vince didn't always pay me to sleep with him, Chris."

"Like I believe anything you say, Connie."

"You can believe whatever the hell you want to. I actually cared about him. He almost made me forget about Ahmad."

"So what made you change your mind?" She turned away from me and mumbled something that was barely audible. "What did you say?"

"I said I got pregnant." I dismissed her with a wave of my hand. I was sick and tired of her lies.

"Don't you get tired of it, Connie?"

"Tired of what?"

"Not being able to tell the truth."

"I'm not lying! The first time you saw me, I was mad as hell, and not just because Vince called me a hoe, but because he didn't want to admit that the baby I had gotten rid of months ago was his." I shook my head and folded my arms, but I waited for her to go on. "Vince wanted me to get rid of it. I figured since Ahmad didn't want me, maybe the baby would bring me and Vince together and we could work something out.

When I told him I didn't want to have the abortion, he told me exactly what he thought of me and said it could be anybody's. Then I guess he got worried that I would hit him up for cash and started throwing a lot of money in my face as a bribe. He convinced me that I could buy some things for my son and asked me if I really wanted to bring another child into this world with the parents being apart. I had the abortion the next day." I felt a little bad that I was going to use the same ploy, but I had my own child to raise, and my marriage was at stake. When I offered her the money, I had to make it look like I wasn't paying her off.

Her feelings were deeper for me than they had been for Vince, and I didn't want to add insult to injury. I decided to reschedule my hotel meeting with Connie.

She beat me to it. "I'm going to keep my room for one more night, and I expect for you to be there by nine p.m." It was not a request.

"What if I can't make that, your highness?" She didn't seem at all affected by my sarcasm.

"Then I'll be very disappointed."

"Disappointed enough to put maxi pads in my car this time?" Connie fiddled with her purse.

"I don't know what you're talking about."

"Yeah, right."

"All you need to know is one thing. If I were the type to do something like that the first time I got really pissed at you, imagine what would happen the next." Connie pulled bobby pins out of her bag and calmly twisted her auburn hair into a sophisticated bun. "Nine p.m.," she said and stalked out of the restaurant.

$$$$

There I was, sneaking around after hours to consummate a deal with Connie that had different terms for the both of us. I had a sinking feeling in my stomach thinking about the lie I had told Sylvia—I was supposed to be working late tonight which was an excuse that wasn't very original. I was actually planning on screwing the devil. Again. I didn't think it would go over well if I just walked into Connie's room, handed over a check, and left—Connie didn't want to be treated like a whore.

I had to convince Connie that I was still attracted to her. But if I could also convince her that my unborn child's well-being was just as important to me as Darren's was to her, maybe she would understand why I had to choose my family. I knew that family was very important to Connie, and hopefully, that angle would work for me and we could both go on with our lives.

I knew that Darren was more important to Connie than anyone else, and I was sure that she would be smart about taking the money if I could make her believe that it wasn't just a bribe.

As I entered the lobby of the Staten Island Hotel, I had the feeling that everyone was pointing their fingers at me as though to say "here he goes again." Between my guilt over Sylvia and my dislike towards Connie, I didn't know which would keep my dick limper tonight. I knocked on Connie's door a few times, not really wanting her to hear me. She swung it open, allowing me to drink up all that she offered. Suffice it to say, I wanted to take more than just a sip. I don't know what the difference was between seeing Connie's naked body draped across my desk the night before and seeing her scantily clad body in front of me right then.

But there was a difference, because it wasn't as difficult as I had presumed to maintain a hard on. It didn't take me long to figure out what had changed—I would have the control tonight. I had come to her room on a mission, and my confidence was back. I planned on fucking her until she sported two crutches.

Her curls were still swept off of her neck and shoulders. The Oriental corset painted across her torso teased me with the imprint of two hardened nipples that threatened to burst through the fabric. She had smothered her shapely legs with baby oil, and the fragrance cascaded into folds I had come to desire months ago and again tonight. Connie took one of my hands and closed the door behind me.

She said nothing and kissed me lightly, like butterfly wings against my mouth. Then she locked her hands behind my neck and kissed me harder, her tongue seemingly searching for my innermost thoughts. I couldn't let Connie gain more leeway than she already thought she had. I sucked on her bottom lip and used my hands to travel the familiar path from the small of her back to the roundness of her ass. I gave it a firm squeeze and Connie released a soft moan that I swallowed hungrily.

I released her mouth, her red lipstick having disappeared, and spun her around. I loosened the strings on the corset as slowly as I could, and I spelled Connie's name across the back of her neck with my tongue. I massaged one of her dark nipples between my thumb and forefinger. I had called them blackberries before, because I had never tasted anything so sweet. I played a soft beat across her clit with my other fingers. Connie began to grind her ass into my groin, attempting to turn and kiss me again. I gently caught her by the shoulders and held her at bay. I cupped one of her breasts in my hand and bent down to take it into my mouth. Connie threw her head back and let out an animalistic sound. First a cub, then a lioness. I didn't ignore the other breast, sucking on it so hard that I thought her delicious juices would spill down my throat. I continued my licking and sucking down her waistline and nibbled on her hips.

I was on my knees moving towards Connie and I backed her onto the bed. Her legs were splayed apart, and I removed her lacy thong with my teeth—after I dragged it over her slim ankles, I made a stop at her painted toes and licked between each one. Connie's milk chocolate called me as I started up her thigh with the taste of baby oil at the roof of my mouth. With no hesitation, I delved my tongue inside of her, and her warm juices coursed down my throat like aged cognac. Connie's legs shook like the thunder they held and she wrapped her thighs around my neck. I placed a finger inside of her and Connie bucked against my hand like a wild horse.

"Chris, this shit feels so good," she moaned.

I knew it did, and I wanted to give her the coup de gras before she came. I stood over her quaking body. I let her watch me as I undressed, and once I was completely naked, Connie reached for my dick. I swiped her hand away and Connie looked at me impatiently. I didn't want her putting her mouth on my dick, because all would be lost. So I removed a condom from my pants on the floor and quickly slipped it on. I took both of Connie's ankles and raised them on either of my shoulders. I lowered myself between her legs and moved the tip inside of her.

"Open your eyes," I ordered.

Connie did as she was told and watched me as I entered her. Connie met each of my thrusts with one of her own and cried on every heavenly being that she could.

Her moans, my moans, and the wetness of our connection were the only sounds to be heard in her room that night.

$$$$

Two hours later, Connie and I were entangled underneath the sheets. I had fallen asleep by mistake. I slid as slowly as I could from the bed and began to dress. Connie stirred and blinked a few times before her eyes focused on me. "Where are you going?" she murmured. I put on my shoes.

"Connie, we need to talk." She sat up immediately, alert to my change of tone.

"About?" I sat at the foot of the bed, not too sure of how Connie was going to react.

"Tonight was great. You brought back a lot of things inside of me that I thought were gone." Connie smiled, but she didn't seem all that happy.

"Why do I feel a 'but' coming on?"

"Because, there is one."

"Don't tell me you're having second thoughts."

"Connie, I was having second thoughts since before I came over here tonight." Connie pulled the sheets up around her, her face burning with shame.

"I wanted you to be very sure about what you were doing before you came over here, Chris. I thought you had come to your senses." I pulled a check for ten thousand dollars out of my wallet and handed it to her. Connie didn't take it, but looked at it like she had never seen one before.

"Connie, in spite of everything we've said and done to each other, I've always had a soft spot for you." That was no longer true, but I knew it was some of what she wanted to hear. "I want you to take this money, and by the end of the month, I'll give you the same amount.

Now, I don't want you to misunderstand what I'm trying to do. As much as I care about you, I need to get my personal life back on track, and so do you. I need to focus on my baby, and you need to do the same, because I know that family is important to you. Because I care about you, I want you to take this check, and maybe, it will make things easier with trying to provide for Darren." Connie lowered her head and shoulders and began to shake. I thought that she didn't want me to see her crying, so I took a step towards her. I jumped when she threw her head back and clapped her hands. She let out a peal of laughter.

"Bravo, Chris," she cried. "Brav-fuckin-o." Connie snatched the check from my hand and ripped it in half, letting it fall to the floor like snowflakes.

"What the hell did you do that for? I'm trying to help you!"

"You're trying to play me is what you're trying to do! You think I'm stupid? You think I actually bought that bullshit you gave me about my son? Well, it was very touching, but no Oscar."

"Someone tries to do something for you so you can have a better life, and this is how you act?"

"This isn't about my life, it's about yours. It always has been. You want the perfect little business, house, car, wife, and baby," she said, checking each one off on her fingers. "Yet, you're here with me risking all of that. I guess you wanna make sure Sylvia gets all the things your drunk ass daddy never gave your mommy. Right, Chris?"

"Shutup," I said. I now regretted all of the personal things I had told Connie after our lovemaking months ago. Connie went to the bathroom and took her robe off the hook on the door. She slipped on her robe and tied it around her waist before giving me one more dirty look as she walked towards the bed. I knew she wasn't done with me yet. Connie put her lips to my ear and whispered softly,

"Don't worry, Chris. Your wife seems pretty happy to me so I doubt she'll put a bullet in her head like your mommy did." I let out a low roar and threw Connie sideways into the wall. A lamp fell off its nightstand and bounced onto the bed—I grabbed her shoulders and threw her onto the bed right along with it. Connie kicked aimlessly, and I caught her ankles and dragged her to me. Her fists were tiny pebbles nicking me as I wrapped my strong hands around her throat and tried to choke her. Her pecan face turned a deep scarlet, and her head flopped back and forth.

I loosened my grip, breathing as raggedly as she was as she clutched her neck. She regained her composure and spit a wad of saliva on my right cheek. I touched the molten liquid and drew my hand back to slap her. A loud rapping at the door stopped me and Connie and I both looked towards the sound. Connie straightened her robe and crawled out from underneath me. She unlocked the door and peeked out.

"Everything all right in there, ma'am?" I heard the male voice ask. It must have been hotel security—the way we were going at it, someone was bound to have heard.

"Yes," Connie said sweetly. "My husband and I, it's our anniversary. Guess we just got carried away. I'm sorry."

"Well, try and keep it down, okay? We just got two complaints."

"Sure, no problem."

Connie turned back to me with her hands on her hips, but I was already prepared to leave before I killed her. "We're not done yet."

"I'm done."

"You know, I thought you were different, but you're trying to treat me like a whore. Just like the rest of them." I nudged Connie out of the way and opened the door. I turned back to her before I decided to leave.

"The offer still stands, if you're willing to take it."

"Well, you didn't offer what I wanted, so now, the stakes have just been raised."

"What's that supposed to mean?"

"It means that payback's a bitch. And her name is Connie."

Chapter 51

I sat in my study, taking a long drag from my cigarette. Moments like this, I was happy that Sylvia had kept a cigarette stash she could no longer smoke due to the pregnancy. She had obviously been angry with me for coming home so late but changed her mind about getting into it with me once she saw the look on my face. She had gone to bed an hour before, and when I heard the knock at the door, I assumed her anger had subsided. To my surprise, Elaine walked in.

I forgot that she had been discharged today. She looked fabulous wearing a snug white sweater and a pair of white seersucker slacks, despite the bandage on her head. Her hair was held in a twist, and she seemed sure of herself but not in a bitchy way. I didn't think that she would try anything funny again, because she left the door open. After all, we hadn't spoken since the incident in the garage. "Chris, you and I have never been close."

I snorted.

"That's for damned sure."

"It was never because I thought you weren't good enough for my daughter."

"Well, you coulda fooled me." Elaine sat on the edge of my desk and gave me a serious look. I started to get uncomfortable again. I wished she would just pick a mood and stick with it. I certainly couldn't deal with another unbalanced woman.

"I already spoke to Sylvia, and I thanked her for what she did. Well, what you two did."

"Which is?" She laughed nervously.

"Things have been different since I met Jonathan . . . I mean my . . . my father. Actually, I've never been happier. It was a big surprise, but one that I needed. So, I guess that's what I'm thanking you for."

"Well, Sylvia was curious about her grandfather's whereabouts too. She also knew that you had been bringing him up a lot lately and thought that it might make you happy to get some closure on that part of your life. So I supported her wishes."

“That’s the other thing I wanted to talk about. I have always known that you would give my daughter the world if she asked. I guess that’s why I hated you so much.” I raised my eyebrows, and she looked away. Elaine focused on the corner of my desk and began to trace circles on it with her fingers.

“As you know, Aldo hasn’t been happy with me for a long time, and most of that stems from my illness.” I was sure that some of it stemmed from his attitude too. “Sometimes, I embarrass him in front of his colleagues and—”

“I’m curious as to why you’re telling me all this, Elaine.”

“Because I’ve always envied you and Sylvia’s relationship.”

“Wait a minute, I never took Sylvia away from you. You two have always been close—”

“I don’t mean like that. I mean the way you treat her,” she blurted out. “Like you love her no matter what.” It all began to come together now. How it seemed like Elaine never had anything positive to say about me, not to mention the snide way she would try to get in between me and Sylvia. She was jealous of her daughter's happiness. "I know that Aldo can be a lot to handle at times, but I know that deep down he loves me, and I love him. I'm sure that he only wants what's best for me." I had heard those words before years ago, and I knew that the only way that Elaine would free herself from Aldo's abuse was to leave him. His word was law and if you didn't abide by it you would find your ass out on the streets just as Sylvia had.

She had found out the hard way when she hadn't become an attorney as he had expected. Sylvia never had to worry though—I would always provide for her in a way that my father had never provided for his wife.

I wanted Sylvia to be happy. It seemed like the only way I could save her the torture of finding out about the affair, was to simply tell her the truth. I just didn't know how yet. It frightened me, because the only chance I had had of getting rid of Connie was when I had gripped her throat until she stopped squirming, stopped breathing. Elaine watched me curiously. I knew that she had said something I missed.

"I'm sorry, what did you say?"

"I was trying to apologize to you, Chris. For the way I've been treating you all these years. For not being happy for my daughter, because I wasn't happy. I haven't been brave enough to tell her that part, so please don't say anything, okay?" I appreciated the apology and nodded my head in agreement. Maybe, Elaine and I could call a truce. "There's something else I wanted to apologize for . . . what I did to you in the garage that day. I was off of my meds, and I wasn't thinking—"

"Elaine, stop. Let's not go there."

"We need to. I feel so guilty, and every time I look at my daughter, I feel sick thinking about how I threw myself at you." Her bottom lip trembled, and her eyes watered over. I had always been a sucker for tears, so I gave her a hug while she sobbed loudly and cried into my shoulder. Neither one of us heard Sylvia's own soft crying at the door.

"You two—" Sylvia started and placed a hand over her mouth. I turned so quickly that Elaine nearly fell on the floor. It didn't take me long to figure out how much Sylvia had heard.

"Sylvia, wait."

"I am so glad I woke up and came down here to apologize for not asking my husband how his day went. What do you want me to wait for, Chris? You and my mom to fuck again?"

Elaine sobbed even louder and held her hand out to her daughter.

"Baby, I am so sorry." Sylvia eyed her in disgust and slapped her hand away.

"I always knew you were a snob, Ma, but I had no idea you were a whore!" I watched in shock as Sylvia shoved her mother, and Elaine's body flipped over my desk and landed on the other side. I threw my hands up not knowing if Sylvia was going to hit me as well. She jabbed her finger at me and headed for the stairs all at the same time.

"You are not even worth it, you lying asshole!"

I chased her up the staircase, surprised at how quickly she moved. She went into the closet, drug out a suitcase, and threw it on the bed.

"What the hell are you doing, Vee?"

"What does it look like? I'm leaving." Sylvia ripped clothes off of hangers and sent them flying out of drawers. I wanted to put them all back where they belonged, but I didn't dare. I didn't know what I would have done if I had heard what she just had. Why the hell did Elaine have to leave that door open?

"You cannot leave in the middle of the night like this. You're pregnant, god-dammit!"

"Well, me and my baby don't want to be here with you and your whore!"

"Sylvia, I love you. I didn't do anything to or with your mother. I stopped her—"

"Oh, so it's her fault because she came on to you, that's it? Because she made the first move? I walked in on you two in that garage quite a while ago, so that means that lying bitch has been living in our house ever since, and you said nothing. To think, I felt sorry for her." Sylvia slammed the suitcase shut and zipped it up. It made a ripping noise just like the one in my chest at that moment. I continued to try and reason with her as she burst through the bedroom door and headed down the stairs, but she ignored me. Sylvia stopped in the foyer catching sight of her disheveled mother exiting my study. Elaine's lower lip was bleeding and she was holding herself, crying uncontrollably.

"Please, Sylvia, don't leave. I'll leave. It wasn't Chris' fault."

Sylvia's voice shook when she spoke, her keys in her hands and tears in her eyes.

"I'll get the rest of my things later." Elaine and I couldn't look at each other after she left. We sat in the kitchen for a half hour, waiting for Sylvia to drive off her anger and come back home. When it got close to three a.m., I had the sinking feeling that I wouldn't have to sleep elsewhere that night, because Sylvia wasn't going to be stepping through the front door.

I had had enough worrying, and I told Elaine that I was going to go looking for her. I told her to stay put just in case Sylvia changed her mind and came back. Sylvia didn't have much of a relationship with her father, but I knew she still wanted one. I decided to try his place first.

$$$$

Aldo's "place" was a like a fortress, set up high on one of the many hills in Staten Island surrounded by a wrought-iron gate. After I entered the code to get onto his property, I drove up the long, cobblestone driveway and parked my car in front of his mansion. I rang the doorbell three times, and Aldo's groggy voice came over the intercom. "What?" he snapped.

"It's Chris." Aldo paused for a moment and laughed harshly.

"I guess you're looking for your wife?"

"Is she here?"

"No, and as usual, my wife has really fucked up." I swallowed hard. So he knew what was going on. I had never feared my father-in-law, but I knew he was a very powerful man. And this was the first time I had crossed him. I had heard the rumors about what he had done to squatters who refused to move from a piece of abandoned property he wanted.

Now, he believed that I had screwed his wife. "I'm not angry with you, Chris, if that's what you're thinking," he said. "A man is going to be a man at the end of the day, so if Elaine offered it, why wouldn't you take it?" I couldn't believe what he was saying to me—it was *alright* to sleep with his wife while his pregnant daughter was who knows where. "Hell, Elaine's body turned me off when she was pregnant, too. I had no choice but to do the same."

"I didn't sleep with your wife, Aldo."

"Apparently, something happened to make my daughter want to come over here in the middle of the night."

"Well, where is she?"

"The hell if I know. I don't have time for the drama right now, Chris. That's why her mother isn't here."

"So, you turned her and your grandchild away?"

"Oh please, Chris. People do have cell phones these days. Be a man and maintain some discipline in your household. Which brings me back to my wife. Just because I'm not angry with you, does not mean that I want to be embarrassed by the fact that she fucked my son-in-law. I will not be made a fool of, so you tell her to get her ass home as soon as you see her again. Have a good night."

Of course I had tried calling Sylvia, but she wasn't answering her phone. I even tried several of her friends and colleagues, but all I got were hang-ups or a bunch of questions I didn't feel like answering. I drove to Clove Lake Park and walked around for about two hours wanting to pull my hair out once I saw the sun sifting through the dense trees. My cell started buzzing, and I saw that someone was trying to call me from my house. It was Elaine, and she was hysterical. "Elaine, slow down, I can't understand you."

"It's all my fault . . ."

"What's all your fault? Is Sylvia home?"

"They took her."

"Who took her?" I asked, my heart pounding in my chest. Elaine gasped for air like a fish out of water.

"Sylvia must have gotten a room at a hotel. A man just called here and said that he broke into her room and that he was going to kill her if you didn't get over there in the next twenty minutes. He taped the hotel key to your front door, so they could still be outside . . . I'm scared, Chris. They have my little girl!"

"Calm down. Which hotel?" Elaine gave me the information, and I told her that I was on my way home. I told her to keep the alarm on and not to leave the house.

"You said 'they.' Was it more than one of them?"

"Some woman got on the phone, too, and she said that you were to come alone and that the police were not to be called."

That was okay, I thought. I didn't want them there when I murdered Connie anyhow.

$$$$

I pulled up to the motel in Newark just over the Goethals Bridge. I knew that Connie was a part of this, but I didn't know whom the gentleman was who had called my house or if they planned on killing me too. I didn't have anything but my fury as a weapon, but by now, I was used to all the bad run-ins I had had in hotel rooms over the last couple of months. My heart quickened when I found the room.

I put my ear to the door and heard nothing. An eerie feeling came over me that maybe Connie had already started her game, and no one was in the room at all. I turned the knob and walked right in. Nobody was there, as I had suspected, but a package waited for me on the bed that looked like a well-wrapped birthday gift. I ripped the paper off and opened the box.

I found two photos inside—one with Sylvia bound and gagged, another of her in the same position with a knife to her belly. I couldn't make out who the hand belonged to that brandished the knife, but it was a slender one encased in a black leather glove. There was a pink letter lying under the photos with white tulips around the borders. I read the quick scrawl, wanting to crumple the letter into a tiny ball as I went over each word. It read:

By now, you are probably aware that I mean business, so I'll be straight to the point. Right now, your wife is on her way home with me. If you would like to keep her and your baby alive, you will wire 500,000 U.S. dollars into the account on the back of this letter within 48 hours. That isn't much time, so I suggest you hustle. If my money arrives even one minute late, I'm going to cut her up into a thousand pieces. If you come with anyone or do something stupid like contacting the police, I'll send those pieces to you one by one. See you then, Chris.

I slowly placed the letter and the pictures back in the box and slumped down on the bed. Then I did something I hadn't done in years—I cried like a baby.

$$$$

I was a Nascar driver as I sped up Aldo's driveway again. Elaine called my phone about ten times in a row, but my only goal was getting the money Connie had requested. This time, Aldo gave me the courtesy of coming to the door.

"I thought I told you to tell Elaine that I wanted her to come home, not for her to call me acting like an idiot!"

"So, she told you already?"

"Told me what? I hung up on her." I walked past him into his enormous library. "Where the hell do you think you're going? Didn't I tell you Sylvia wasn't here?"

"Listen to me, Aldo. I know she isn't here."

"If you know she isn't here then why the hell—"

"Just shut the fuck up!" I exploded. Aldo's jaw dropped in disbelief, and he stepped back. "Your daughter could be in serious danger, and I need your help." He watched with no words as I slammed the package down on his desk and ripped the lid off. I shoved the photos into his hand but slipped Connie's letter into my back pocket. If I wanted him to give me the money without wanting to kill me, I had to make him believe that I wasn't at fault for Sylvia's kidnapping. It was a shame that this was what it took to get him involved with his daughter's disappearance.

His bulging hands shook, and he dropped the pictures onto the floor.

"What is this?"

"Someone came by the motel room that Sylvia was staying in tonight, and they took her. They asked for a ransom."

"How much?"

"Half a mil. And they want it by Friday."

I thought up a good story on the way over, and Aldo believed it. I told him that a man had called our home and spoken with Elaine. I told him that the man had left a letter at the motel where I had picked up the box—it read that he and his family had been squatters on a piece of property Aldo had kicked them out of. Now, this guy was getting his revenge. He wanted me, and only me, to deliver the money.

"Any idea who the sonafabitch is?"

"No. But he did make one thing clear, and I don't need to go into any more details than these pictures already have." Aldo placed his hands on his desk and turned his back to me.

"I'm going to get dressed, and I'll be heading to the bank as soon as it opens." Finally, Aldo turned to me, his eyes as dry as the desert sands. "If you get even one chance, you put that asshole in a body bag." I knew then that it wasn't as much about Sylvia as it was about someone fucking over Aldo.

Chapter 52

Connie had gone too far. No one fucked with a man's family. I couldn't wait to get off of that plane and see her again so that I could finish what I had started. I now regretted not having killed her when I had the chance. Thank God I was able to get a plane ticket at the last minute. Once I reached Norfolk International Airport, I searched for a taxi. I flagged down a Yellow Cab, and the grungy, white driver made a sound that resembled "where are you going?"

I had called Vince before I flew out of Jersey and told him that I needed to stay the night. He asked me what this last minute trip was all about, but all I could say was that I would tell him later. Vince was out having brunch with a client, and instead of placing his key under the mat, he had taped it under his mailbox along with the code for his new ADT system—someone had tried to break into his house about a week before. He had also purchased a gun. That was my other reason for coming to his house. I wasn't going to this vague address Connie had given me to pick up my wife without some form of protection. I didn't want to bring my cousin along to get Sylvia, so I figured I would take the gun while he wasn't home. Vince had always been a big mouth, so of course he bragged to me about buying the piece and where he hid it in his room for the next asshole who wanted to try him.

I climbed the stairs to his room and flipped on the light in his walk-in closet. I spotted the slate-gray, Roberto Cavalli shoebox sitting up on the highest shelf. I extended my arm and pulled it out carefully so that I wouldn't knock down the rest of his expensive shoes. I took the box into the guest room and sat on the floor. My hand shook when I opened the box, revealing the automatic 40.0 caliber.

If I was going to bring this metal monster with me, I had to be prepared to use it. I placed the gun under the bed, and lay down with my clothes on. Even though I hadn't slept all night, there was no point in me closing my eyes, because I had too much on my mind.

$$$$

Eventually, I got up after a few hours, because the room began to close in on me. I had on the same clothes since the night before, and I hadn't brought any bags. It was a good thing Vince went straight to his room when he came home, because I knew I looked and smelled terrible. Apparently, his client wasn't just a client—I had to step over her bra and panties in the hallway. I put on one of Vince's robes that was in the bathroom and went downstairs to wash the clothes I wore. Afterwards, I must have fallen asleep on the couch, because the next thing I knew, it was evening by the time Vince woke me up.

"What's going on, Chris?" He shot me a worried glance and went to make himself a sandwich in the kitchen. "You look terrible." I said nothing and focused my eyes on the floor. "Are you and Sylvia okay?" Sylvia, Sylvia, Sylvia.

Who knew where she was or the sick things Connie was doing to her. In a way, Connie had already killed me. She had managed to take something away from me that meant more to me than life itself. To do something as stupid as going to bed with her had only added fuel to the fire. I had thought I was the one in control, that I could manipulate her body and mind and then give her a nice "going away" package. But she was a master manipulator and could spot another one a mile away.

I ignored Vince and went to get dressed. The ticking of the clock in the guestroom would be a throbbing pain in my head until I received Connie's phone call stating that she had received the money. I sat in my room and cried for another hour, visions of Connie stabbing Gary coming to mind. Visions of her doing the same thing to Sylvia. I was just as dirty as she was. I had helped her get rid of the body. Maybe, God was punishing me for that sin, and now, I had to pay Him back, too.

I would never see my baby grow up . . . I knocked over Vince's lamp with the side of my fist and watched the porcelain scatter across the floor. Tiny spots of blood appeared on the side of my hand, but I didn't flinch. I imagined that it was Connie's blood. I knew then that I was ready to pull the trigger if need be. That's how much rage the bitch had instilled in me. Vince burst through the door. He looked at his lamp on the floor and placed his hands on top of his head.

"My two thousand dollar lamp . . . what the hell is it doing in pieces on the floor?" I studied the red flecks on my hand and took a tissue from the night-stand to pat my blotchy skin. He shook his head.

"This guy. Unbelievable. You break my fucking lamp, and you have nothing to say. You know, I really hope you're not down here again for that bitch, Connie." Speak of the devil and she shall appear, because at that very moment, my phone started ringing. The number didn't show on my caller i.d., but I knew who it was. Her voice was as wispy as a feather against my eardrum.

"That was pretty fast, Chris. Good boy. You can collect your prize at nine p.m. tonight. Remember to come alone." I turned to Vince after she hung up.

"I have to borrow your car tonight."

"Now, he speaks."

"I'm sorry about the lamp, Vince. I'll give you whatever it cost."

"I need to know why you knocked it on the floor in the first place."

"I can't talk about it right now."

"Well, you need to talk to somebody, because you look like you're going out of your fucking mind."

"Look, are you gonna let me use your car or not?" Vince released a deep sigh and put a hand on my shoulder.

"Whatever you're about to do, just be careful, alright?" I put my hand atop his and gave it a hard squeeze. By the time the night was over, he might just be looking at me in a coffin.

"Thanks."

$$$$

I walked the beach for a few hours, preparing myself for the danger I could possibly encounter. One glance at my watch, and I knew it was time to face the inevitable. My late uncle Dominic always told me that there were some people in life you had to get rid of to be rid of. The ones who would latch onto you like a leech and suck all the life right out of you. I never agreed with him until I met one of those people.

$$$$

I followed the interstate towards Norfolk as my Mapquest directions had suggested. The directions were remotely familiar to me. I knew that Connie's house was somewhere nearby. Different streets always had a certain smell to them. I slowed down as I approached a dingy, gray, brick building surrounded by a gravel parking lot. It was actually a white building but had probably turned that color after having been abandoned for so many years. I didn't like how this felt at all.

I had come at exactly nine p.m. as Connie had instructed, and there were no cars to be found.

I turned off the headlights as I pulled into the lot. The gun rested comfortably against the small of my back. The cold air sliced my bare face as I stepped out of the car. A dog growled somewhere in the darkness and fought to tear through the chain-link fence behind the back of the building. A couple of steps closer and I realized that it was an old garage Connie had brought me to. Piss had been used as graffiti on the walls, and the stench suffocated me. The thought suddenly occurred to me that Connie and her partner might not even be in there.

They may have left Sylvia in there alone. She could be hurt or freezing to death. I didn't think I would be able to lift the rusted garage doors, so I rounded the building in search of another form of entry. There was a door on the side of the building, but its windows had been covered up with cardboard. I didn't know who or what was waiting for me on the other side, but I braced myself for the worst. I turned the knob, and the door caught. I pressed my weight against it, and it eased open. The creaking hinges were an alarm for anyone that might be waiting for me. I longed for the urine-saturated air outside when I smelled what was in there. I held my hands out in front of me to feel my way through the blackness. I stumbled over something that could have been a cinderblock, and I hit the concrete floor. The dust rose up into my mouth, and I started hacking.

"Sylvia?" I whispered. That stupid dog wouldn't shut up outside. "Sylvia?"

“No,” came the voice out of the darkness. She turned on a fluorescent light overhead, and my eyes took a moment to adjust to the sudden change. There were cinderblocks placed inconspicuously across the floor and tall rusty shelves against the wall held equally rusty cans and tools. The rest of the room was bare besides the beautiful woman sitting in the middle of it. Connie stood up from her folded chair looking completely out of place. She had on a brown page-boy hat and a cream sweater dress. The sound of the heels on her knee-high boots drowned out the barking dog as she came towards me. “Stand up, Chris. I want to get a good look at you.”

I rose slowly and snarled, “Where’s my wife?” Connie put a finger to her chin and looked skyward.

“There’s been a slight change of plans.” I quickly whipped the gun from the small of my back and pointed it at her.

“Don’t fuck with me, Connie. Where is she?” Connie never flinched.

"Are you gonna blow my pretty head off, Chris? Wouldn't be the first time you've seen that."

"Stop fucking with me, and tell me where she is!"

"It's time," she said, looking past me. I turned just as a pair of hands grabbed me on either of my arms. I hadn't even heard them come up behind me. One wrestled the gun from my hand while the other threw me to the ground. He dug his heel into my back and Connie knelt down to smooth back my hair. She lifted my chin and slipped her tongue inside my mouth.

"You thought you were dealing with some stupid hoe from the ghetto, but you were wrong, Chris. Your love alone could have rescued me, but you couldn't even give me that. Now, who's gonna rescue you?" She stood and walked towards the door I had just come through. "He's all yours," she said to the two thugs standing atop me. "Oh, and Chris, baby, I put your wife at the bottom of the Chesapeake Bay. But don't worry, you'll join her in a couple of hours." It took my ears a while to register what she had said before she left.

"Noooo!" I screamed until my lungs bled. I fought to get up, but that sharp blow stole my strength. Sylvia was dead. My baby was dead. I wanted to be dead. The two men weren't going to make it easy though. I was pretty sure that Connie wanted them to do a job on me. They dragged me on my knees to the chair Connie had been sitting in. It was still warm, but I didn't want to feel anything, and my tears blinded me. My Vee. She was gone. She had paid for my mistakes after all. My head hung low as the two black men tied me to the chair. I didn't recognize either one of them and didn't care to. One of them grabbed a bucket from the floor and dumped its ice-cold water on top of my head. I let out a yelp and shivered as my clothes molded to my body.

"That's it, mothafucka," one of them said. "We want you to feel this shit." The other one went over to the shelf against the wall and grabbed a wrench about the size of my forearm. He stood next to me and cocked his arm back like he was wielding a golf club. The wrench made a dull noise as it hit me just behind my left ear. My head jerked forward, and I felt a warm liquid dribble down the back of my neck. The room spun, and he drew his hand back again. The second time he hit me, I blacked out.

Chapter 53

So there I was, lying naked in this backseat. I could smell the fresh leather and a twinge of Vince's cologne, so I assumed they had put me back inside of his car. My head throbbed until the pain grew overbearing, and my hair was matted to the side of my face. I wretched twice as I lay on my side and fought back the nausea from the blood I swallowed.

The blindfold rested diagonally across my face from all the twisting and turning I had done, and I blacked out several times in between. I still saw a glare from the fluorescent light, so I knew they hadn't moved me to a different location. I heard the muffled voices of two men talking in the distance. With everything I had in me, I lifted my head above the window to find out where they were.

There wasn't enough strength in my neck to raise my head high enough to see their faces, so all I could make out were two pair of feet at the door. The one wearing the tan, ostrich-skin shoes walked outside while a pair of white sneakers came towards me. I slumped down and instantly vomited. Although the smell made me even sicker, I lay stiff as a log. He opened the right rear door, and half of my body fell out.

"What the hell? Awww shit, you gotta be kiddin' me," he said. "How the hell we supposed to strip this bitch and you done threw up in her?" He kicked me in my side, and when I didn't move, he pulled me from the car. I felt him loosening the twine around my wrists and ankles, and he removed my blindfold. I smelled the tobacco on his breath as he leaned down and licked the back of my ear. "I'm gonna hose this bitch down, and then, I'm gonna give you some of my hose for being such a bad boy."

As soon as I heard him go outside, I sat up on my elbows and used the open car door to pull myself up. I staggered over to the shelf that held the wrench they had beaten me with. Instead of rust, it was now caked in my blood. I took it and moved towards the door in a blur. I leaned against the wall next to the door, praying that I didn't lose consciousness again. The tall, peanut-colored man burst through the door with a hose in his hands and gave the empty floor a vexed look.

His eyes widened, and he looked over at me as I swung the wrench.

$$$$

I sped through the dim narrow streets with my captor's clothes on. The man had struck the floor like lightning, and after I was through with him, his white collar had turned a maroon color. I cruised the streets in a car that smelled vaguely of the vomit I had cleaned up. I didn't care—I just wanted Connie's head on a stick. I drove down a street by the name of Hardy Avenue, and for a second, I thought I was home on Staten Island. I had the same adrenaline coursing through my blood as I did the day Baldy had chased me down, so I knew that Connie's home was nearby. This time, she wouldn't have her bodyguards standing in between us, and I would tear her—

A teenager dashed in front of the car wearing a black t-shirt and jeans. I slammed on my brakes and turned the wheel while the tires squealed. The car narrowly missed him, and the fender clipped one of his thighs. The boy rolled across the street, and the two young men who were apparently chasing him stopped in their tracks. I got out of the car to make sure he was okay and stepped into the brightness of Vince's headlights. The teenager on the ground looked at the other two fearfully, and I turned to them. Once they caught one look at my battered head and bloody shirt, they hesitated and ran their separate ways. I extended my hand to the kid, but he backed away from me on the heels of his palms and feet. He panted uncontrollably, and I was sure that I had put the fear of God into him. I squinted my blackened eyes and tilted my head in recognition. He didn't know who I was behind this distorted mask.

"I know you."

"I don't know *you*."

"I bet you remember the money I gave you." The kid took a closer look, and his eyes got real big.

"Oh shit, white boy? They really fucked you up this time."

"Not the guys that jumped me that day."

The kid stood up and dusted himselfoff.

"You and Connie still friends?"

"We got unfinished business."

"Yeah?"

"Yeah. But I need you to remind me of where she lives."

"Aight, but it might cost you again."

"No problem." The kid got into the car and brought me to her house which happened to be two blocks away. I staggered around the car and stopped short of the "for sale" sign. I stepped over it and walked up the steps. My puffy eyes peered into each of the windows that hovered over the veranda. The house was dark, but I could see that the furniture was gone. A strong burst of revelation helped me down those steps with a sudden speed. I opened the passenger door of Vince's car and snatched the kid out by his collar.

"Why didn't you tell me she left?" Even though he tried to keep a hardened face, there was fear in his eyes. His expression melted like butter.

"I thought you knew man, leggo!" My chest rose and fell heavily, and I loosened my grip on him. "Fuck the money—

you crazy! I'm out." The kid took off in the opposite direction, but this time, he didn't glance over his shoulder. I needed to find Connie like a junkie needed a hit. Sylvia's bloated body would probably be found floating in the water and Connie would be somewhere enjoying a mimosa. I would go home empty-handed and break the news to friends and family that they would never see Sylvia again, because I had fucked around. Connie would spend Aldo's money in Negril or Paris maybe . . . The thought occurred to me that Vince might have an idea of where Connie had run off to. Maybe, over the course of their relationship, she had revealed a special place to him just as I had revealed my secrets to her. Without the kid, I would have to find my own way back.

$$$$

Vince was asleep on the couch when I returned. I knew it wasn't a good idea to keep carrying around the gun, so I immediately went to put it away. The darkness of his room kept me from having to look at myself in the mirror. I flipped on the light in his walk-in closet and searched for the gray shoebox. I found it and set the gun on the floor while I reached for its container. As I pulled the box out, I accidentally nudged a few others, and they toppled to the floor. I put the gun in the Cavalli box and went to work putting the other shoe boxes back on their shelves—I didn't want Vince knowing I had his gun in the first place. One particular pair of shoes caught my eye that had fallen away from the others. They were a caramel color, almost tan. They were very nice and clearly expensive. Ostrich-skin. My heart quickened a pace, and I dropped whatever had been in my hands.

Chapter 54

When Vince's eyes opened, I was standing in front of him with my fists at my sides. It took him a moment to realize it was me, and I was surprised at how calm I was. Vince's mouth opened in a weirdly shaped "o," and he wrinkled his brow.

"Chr . . . Chris? What happened?" If I had never found out he had been there, I would have thought he was asking out of concern. What he really wanted to know was how I had made it out of there alive.

"I was beaten," I said quietly. "Almost to fucking death." I watched the way his face twitched and the muscles moved in his throat. Vince looked over at the wall, his eyes darting back and forth as he searched for the role of the concerned cousin.

"Why?" He put his hand on my shoulder, and I shrunk back.

"That's what I'm trying to find out."

"There's blood all over you. I'm calling 911."

Vince turned his back to me and went to lift the receiver from its cradle. I pulled the gun from the small of my back. My voice was the dangerous rattle of a snake.

"Why? You never finished the job."

Vince paused and put the phone down. "What?" he said. He turned his head just enough to see the gun at my side. He spun around to face me then.

"Why were you there, Vince?"

"Chris, what are you—" I aimed the gun at him. My body shook, but my hand was steady.

"Don't you even fucking lie to me! I saw you at the garage. Now where the fuck is Connie?" His hazel eyes flickered, and all it took was a few seconds for them to sink as shallow as water.

"She was mine before she was yours." I kept shaking my head over and over, already on the brink of insanity.

"You tried to kill me over that whore? And what about Sylvia, you piece of shit, what did she ever do to you?"

"I'm talking about Sylvia!" he screamed. I put my hand on my temple and kept the gun on him with the other. I stepped back.

"What did you say?"

"Let me explain, you dumb fuck. Sylvia and I met in college. We dated off and on for two years before her father decided he wanted her at a better school. She couldn't say no to him, so she left me. I didn't see her again until you two started dating. I was in love with her then and that never changed. Not even when she made the mistake of marrying you."

I wasn't breathing properly. He was lying of course. Wasn't he? Sylvia and Vince couldn't stand each other. They barely spoke. She would have told me they dated, right? She wouldn't have kept something like that inside for too long. She was honest. She loved me too much not to be. I thought of the way she tensed up whenever I mentioned my cousin's name, how she grew quiet and averted her green eyes. No, she hated him. He was a liar.

"Don't try to figure it out, Chris," he said, reading my mind. "There's nothing to figure out. You thought you were this great husband but you started paying more attention to that stupid restaurant than you did her." He didn't know Sylvia like I had. He had never touched her like I had. Liar. Filthy, fucking liar. "I wanted to *kill* you when she told me you slapped the shit outta her. Turning out to be just like your old man, huh?" *Be quiet, Vince*, I thought. *Be quiet so I won't have to kill you.* "And that car—you had to go and be just like me didn't you . . . it felt so good scratching it the fuck up. On top of that, you had to have my woman, too."

"You shut your fucking mouth! You think you would have been better for her, running around fucking everything that breathes?"

"I never gave a shit about any of those bitches! I was just biding my time until Sylvia became mine. I was so pissed off, sooo pissed off, when those idiots burned down the restaurant, because only then did your ass decide to go back home, and I had to picture you with her again. I had no choice but to hurry up and get rid of you, because there was no way in hell you were raising our baby." That one cut me deeper than a machete.

"No," I mouthed, my steady hand growing weaker. The baby I had listened to and cried for had been Vince's? I couldn't take anymore. Vince started walking towards me, wearing his usual smirk.

But this one didn't suggest fun and games.

"That's right, Chris. *My* baby. Remember when I took that business trip to New York? I was really fucking Sylvia in your king-sized bed on your royal-blue satin sheets. I came inside of her, and I made her cry. She told me she had forgotten the last time you made her do that." He pressed a button in my head, and I wrapped both hands around the gun. I cocked it. With my finger crooked comfortably over the trigger, I pulled. Nothing, so I pulled again. Still, no shot rang out. Vince stopped walking and cocked his head to the side. "I didn't realize I had forgotten my gun. Too bad you didn't make sure it was loaded."

I looked at the gun, and Vince lunged at me. He was small in stature but attacked like a pitbull. My body ached all over and Vince made it worse by delivering fierce blows to my head and ribs. I almost lost my footing as he pummeled me, and the corner of an end table sliced into my thigh. I grabbed the lamp from the end table and swung it at him, but he ducked. He was too fast for me. He backed away, and I knew then that I had him with my reach. I gave him a left jab, and his head snapped back. Vince touched his open lip and a thin line of blood slid down his chin. I wanted to see more. I thought of my dead wife, their betrayal, and the baby that wasn't mine. Vince wobbled back and forth after a series of my punches, and I rammed into his chest with one of my shoulders. I sent him flying and he fell through the screen door onto his balcony.

He attempted to stand. I pulled him up by his collar and slammed my fist into his chin, nearly knocking him off his feet. His arms flailed about making circles in the air as he tried to catch his balance. I gave him a second shove and he flipped over the side of the balcony. Three seconds. That was how long one of his hands held onto the railing. Each finger slipped off one by one. "Aaagh!" he cried . . . until his neck snapped against the grill on the wooden deck below. It was the last sound I heard out of him.

A woman was walking her dog a couple yards away, and the poodle started yipping like crazy. Her pale, freckled face turned as red as her hair and she screamed. "He pushed him! Oh my God, he pushed him. Somebody call the police!"

Two years later...

Today, everything is a blur to me. Today is the day Sylvia died. Even after all this time has passed, I can't forget how I felt that day. Our love had seemingly flowed like fresh water, but she tainted that love with the impurity of her betrayal. Their betrayal. The two people I had cared for the most are the two I can never forgive. Everyday I spend in this shithole is a reminder.

When the judge sentenced me to fifteen years, my attorney was the only one who wouldn't look at me. Aldo had never stopped. Karen, whom the prosecutor had found as a witness to testify, revealed the fact that Sylvia and Vince were indeed having an affair—even when she and Sylvia worked together, because I was supposedly never around.

Aldo was convinced, much like everyone else, that I had killed my cousin and perhaps my wife out of sheer jealousy—he thought I had gone to Vince's place looking for trouble, a terrible fight had followed, and I had thrown Vince to his death. Aldo also believed that I was responsible for the disappearance of his money. Although it had been wired to an undisclosed account, he assumed I was working with someone and was to meet up with them after I had gotten rid of Sylvia and Vince—supposedly, I had the misfortune of getting caught.

It sounded like a great idea that was pieced together as neatly as a jigsaw puzzle, but it wasn't true. Aldo didn't want me in prison, because he wanted to kill me himself.

Elaine had been taken out of court for trying to slap me during the trial. I couldn't believe that even Carla, who had been like a sister to me, thought I had killed my wife despite having seen how crazy Connie was. She refused to listen to my story about the real murderer. I lost Sylvia, the respect of my colleagues, and my restaurant after all. Not because I had fucked Connie, but because she had fucked me.

I was charged with second degree murder for killing my cousin. I was implicated in Sylvia's death, too, but they couldn't find her body. Connie got away, and here I am, nothing more than a number for several years to come.

Today is different in one way though. The young kid that hands out the mail paid me a visit, and usually, I never get anything. When he placed it in my hand I frowned, realizing there was nothing written on the postcard besides my name. I slowly turned it over, and my heart stopped. There was a picture of a gondola along the river in Venice—I had proposed to *her* there.

Epilogue

My name is Constance Michelle Green. Some people still refer to me as Candy. I met Vince a couple of years ago when he was running the streets with my Uncle Gary. An unlikely pair? Hardly. Vince and Gary had two things in common—women and gambling. Vince and I quickly became friends inside and outside of the bed. I found refuge at his home away from Gary's "hand problem," and I was his confidante on those late nights he went on and on about the woman he could never have.

Who knew she was his cousin's wife? I certainly didn't until Sylvia called Vince's house one morning after he had already left for work. He and I had been drinking the night before, and I was still trying to pull myself from his crisp sheets. She promptly cursed me out, and I cursed her back.

I told her that I had no idea Vince was involved with anyone, let alone the mystery woman he always spoke of. I heard the passion in her tone, and I must say I felt sorry for her considering the passionate feelings I still had for Ahmad. After all, my main goal was to get Ahmad back into my arms and give Darren the family he deserved. But I couldn't do that in Virginia. I needed the money Vince was giving me to get the hell out of Virginia and away from Gary. So, I decided to use this Sylvia situation to my advantage.

She had stopped sleeping with her husband to appease Vince, but Vince hadn't kept his end of the bargain—he couldn't seem to keep Mr. Happy in his pants. But I promised her that I wouldn't sleep with Vince anymore and that I would keep an eye on him. After all, she planned on calling it off with her husband if Vince had truly changed and wasn't the same ladies' man he had been in college.

I guess she was just as weak as the rest of us chicks when it comes to first loves, even the assholes. She paid me a couple hundred every month for my spying. Vince and I remained platonic friends, and he was cool with that, though he made a pass at me every now and then. He kept complaining to me that he couldn't stand seeing Sylvia and Chris together any longer. He told me that he and Sylvia had come up with a plan for them to be together and pay back her asshole of a father all at the same time. Vince had convinced me that he would pay me a great deal of money if I agreed to be a part of their scheme.

He had no idea that Sylvia and I had been speaking almost every day or that she was already paying me for the "service" I provided.

Vince assured me that Chris had a weakness for victimized women. He said it was because Chris was too young to stop his mother's relentless beatings. But in Sylvia's eyes, Chris had started to become just as controlling as his father, the very reason she left her own father's house to begin with. I lured Chris with my abused act, though it wasn't completely an act, and he fell for it.

The idea was to make Chris believe that I would be crazy enough to kidnap his wife for a ransom—after he dropped me like a bad habit. It was just a matter of good timing. We were going to get rid of him when he came looking for her. I would collect my cut later, and Sylvia and

Vince could move on with their lives in another city.

None of us expected Chris to escape and kill Vince. But don't get it twisted, Sylvia didn't shed one tear for Vince. I had already informed her, weeks before the plan was to take place, that I had seen him kissing some big-tittied blonde as she exited his condo. Sylvia said if he ever broke her heart again, she would break his neck. So she planned to get rid of him, too, and split the money fifty-fifty with me. She turned out to be pretty cool.

She was as sick of these tired men as I was, and she actually helped me trick Chris into thinking Gary was sicker than he already had been. The dead cat she left on my car had even shocked me. If she hadn't done that, maybc Chris wouldn't have thought my life was in danger, and he wouldn't have come to my rescue the night Gary died—I knew I wouldn't be able to take Gary down by myself.

When Sylvia planted those tampons in Chris' car using a spare set of keys, I gave her the thumbs up sign. As for Elaine, she had come to the conclusion a long time ago that she had to get away from her husband as well. She and Sylvia can't stop laughing whenever they talk about Sylvia planning to walk in on that conversation that landed Elaine on the other side of Chris' desk.

Elaine walked out on her husband after the trial and didn't bat an eyelash when he told her she would be nothing without him. Hell, she would still spend his money with her daughter and Aldo wouldn't even know it. Jonathan Dollar is now the new man in Elaine's life and calls his daughter to tell her how much he loves her every week. Sylvia and Elaine now live near a cousin in Italy under completely different names, and only Mr. Dollar and I know that.

I have a beautiful picture of her daughter, Sophie, whom Darren has a crush on. Gary left the house to me, and I sold it after his death.

I used the money to buy a condo in Atlanta and finish my degree. After Ahmad realized I was trying to clean up my act, he gave me joint custody of Darren. My son comes to live with me during the summer, and when Ahmad brought him here last Christmas, we realized our chemistry was still there. He's even thinking of transferring here through his company . . .

Someone once said that assholes rule the world, but I found out that a bitch can control the universe. I look out over the skyline and raise my mimosa towards the clouds.

It's a toast to all my powerful women. Cheers.

About the Author…

This is Alicia Coston's first novel. In her spare time, she mentors at-risk youth and also sings as Lanae Jewalz in the male/female hip-hop duo, DiverCity. Her future goal is to create a fine arts program for inner-city kids. She currently resides in Virginia Beach, Virginia with her husband and is working on her second novel.